J Howlett-Ross

A Memoir of the Life of Adam Lindsay Gordon

J Howlett-Ross

A Memoir of the Life of Adam Lindsay Gordon

ISBN/EAN: 9783744693394

Printed in Europe, USA, Canada, Australia, Japan

Cover: Foto ©Raphael Reischuk / pixelio.de

More available books at **www.hansebooks.com**

THE LAUREATE OF THE CENTAURS:

A MEMOIR OF THE LIFE OF

ADAM LINDSAY GORDON.

The Gresham Press,

UNWIN BROTHERS,

CHILWORTH AND LONDON.

To my Mother.

ADAM LINDSAY GORDON.

BORN 1833, DIED 1870

A MEMOIR OF THE LIFE OF

ADAM LINDSAY GORDON

The "Laureate of the Centaurs"

WITH

*NEW POEMS, PROSE SKETCHES, POLITICAL SPEECHES
AND REMINISCENCES, AND AN "IN MEMORIAM"
BY KENDALL*

BY

J. HOWLETT-ROSS

WITH PORTRAIT

London
WILLIAM W. GIBBINGS
18, BURY STREET, W.C.
1892

NOTE.

I HAVE to acknowledge my indebtedness to the proprietors of the *Australasian* for permission to use the prose sketches; and to able and appreciative articles by Mr. A. Sutherland, M.A., and the Rev. E. Tenison Woods. Much information has been gleaned from old newspapers and from personal friends of the poet, and every effort made to give the fullest obtainable information of Australia's " Poet Laureate of the Centaurs."

CONTENTS.

IN MEMORIAM.

(A. L. GORDON.)

AT rest ! Hard by the margin of that sea
Whose sounds are mingled with his noble verse,
Now lies the shell that never more will house
The fine, strong spirit of my gifted friend.
Yea, he who flashed upon us suddenly,
A shining soul with syllables of fire,
Who sang the first great songs these lands can claim
To be their own ; the one who did not seem
To know what royal place awaited him
Within the Temple of the Beautiful,
Has passed away ; and we who knew him, sit
Aghast in darkness, dumb with that great grief,
Whose stature yet we cannot comprehend ;
While over yonder churchyard, hearsed with pines,
The nightwind sings its immemorial hymn,
And sobs above a newly-covered grave.

The bard, the scholar, and the man who lived
That frank, that open-hearted life which keeps
The splendid fire of English chivalry
From dying out ; the one who never wronged
A fellowman ; the faithful friend who judged
The many, anxious to be loved of him,
By what he saw, and not by what he heard,
As lesser spirits do ; the brave great soul
That never told a lie, or turned aside
To fly from danger ; he, I say, was one

Of that bright company this sin-stained world
Can ill afford to lose.

       They did not know,
The hundreds who had read his sturdy verse
And revelled over ringing major notes,
The mournful meaning of the undersong
Which runs through all he wrote, and often takes
The deep autumnal, half-prophetic tone
Of forest winds in March ; nor did they think
That on that healthy-hearted man there lay
The wild specific curse which seems to cling
For ever to the Poet's twofold life !

To Adam Lindsay Gordon, I who laid
Two years ago on Lionel Michael's grave
A tender leaf of my regard ; yea I,
Who culled a garland from the flowers of song
To place where Harpur sleeps ; I, left alone,
The sad disciple of a shining band
Now gone ! to Adam Lindsay Gordon's name
I dedicate these lines ; and if 'tis true
That, past the darkness of the grave, the soul
Becomes omniscient, then the bard may stoop
From his high seat to take the offering,
And read it with a sigh for human friends,
In human bonds, and gray with human griefs.

And having wove and proffered this poor wreath,
I stand to-day as lone as he who saw
At nightfall through the glimmering moony mists,
The last of Arthur on the wailing mere,
And strained in vain to hear the going voice.

                 HENRY KENDALL.

ADAM LINDSAY GORDON.

A Memoir.

—∗∗—

MANY years have elapsed since the death of Adam
Lindsay Gordon—a name that is companion to
many loved memories of the past, and recalls with
fond regret the absence of a royal spirit, so gifted,
so human, and so unfortunate. Cut off in the
zenith of his splendid powers, snatched away on
the threshold of fame, fortune, and happiness,
destroyed by the same hand that gave us the too
insufficient evidences left of his superb faculties,
Adam Lindsay Gordon remains to us a noble
memory, sanctified by the awful baptism of death,
hallowed by the tenderest thoughts of an abiding
friendship, and illuminated by the glorious genius
of a fine, fearless, kingly nature.

Year by year, as the fame of the poet has taken
deeper and wider hold upon the hearts of the

people, so has the desire to know more of his
chequered life and his untimely death grown in
intensity, and much disappointment has been felt
by the admirers of " poor Gordon," as Australians
lovingly call him, that hitherto no edition of his
works has contained anything of a biographical
nature beyond the few lines of reference in
Marcus Clarke's sympathetic and elegantly
written preface. It is hoped the present memoir
will supply a demand, which, reasonable in itself,
proves also the deep love and sincere admiration
that Australians have for the ablest interpreter of
a phase of life that may be held to be essentially
Australian. So eventful was the career, so erratic
the genius, and so honourable the character of the
unfortunate poet, that his memory will ever be
lovingly cherished, alike for the glorious legacy of
his verse and the fame of his daring horsemanship. His independent spirit, his enthusiastic
love of sport, and his untimely end struck strong
chords of sympathy in the hearts of the Australian people, whose independence and athleticism
are world-famous. He has been well described
as one of those gifted men whose intellectual
powers are imperfectly known to themselves, and
only partially revealed to the world, owing to a
feeling of hesitation and self-distrust on the part
of their possessors, and to a shy and hesitating

manner, which is liable to be misinterpreted as an indication of mental weakness or poverty by superficial observers. Gordon combined the simplicity and modesty of genius with its fire and force. It can be imagined that if one of the fabulous centaurs of Greece could have written poetry, it would have been characterized by the same exuberance of animal life, the same swinging diction, and the same joyous sympathy with the loveliness of nature which are so apparent in the poet's verse.

In general build, Gordon was tall and gaunt, with a stoop in his gait that was attributed to his short-sightedness. An enthusiastic friend once described him as "looking like an ancient Viking, and riding like an Assyrian of old;" and, though always neatly dressed in the bush costume of a slouch hat, blue "jumper" tucked in at the waist, and Wellington boots, he carried the air of a gentleman. His appearance, though eccentric, was fascinating, and commanded respect. He had a large, well-formed head, covered with short, curly, brown hair, and a pale complexion, and the whole contour of his face, says the Rev. E. T. Woods, "reminded one a good deal of the portraits of Byron." His clean-shaven mouth and chin and side whiskers "bespoke the Britisher of his day," says a popular journalist. His eyes had a

wild, haunting look, and when he was terribly in
earnest they seemed to look into one's very soul.
Mr. Hammersley, who knew him well, declares
that at times he was the strangest and most mysterious man he ever saw, one of whom he could
not help feeling afraid, and yet so fascinating
withal as to make it a pleasure to be in his
company. At times he was cheerful and spirited;
at others, moody, melancholy, and despairing.
He was kind, generous, and brave; but his
thoughtful, reserved manner, and habit of riding
by himself during his first years in Australia,
caused him to be considered unsociable. This
supposed unsociableness was not a defect in
disposition, but was rather the result of thought-
fulness and a natural reserve unaccompanied
by either superciliousness or hauteur. He
missed in his bush life the congenial com-
panionship of his early years, and his bold, independent spirit often chafed under the slights
unintentionally put upon it by men whose
birth and education were much beneath that of
the unheeded stockrider. On the stations where
he was employed he was, though not absolutely
a favourite, always well liked for his quiet,
obliging ways, his sobriety, and abstinence from
gambling. Another gentleman, Theo. Carey,
Esq., of Adelaide, describes him as " tall,

thin, swarthy, silent, nervous — apparently morose, except to the few before whom he might unbosom. The mistake of his life was in choosing so largely, and so long, the rough life and associations of the bush, in *those evil times*, which unfitted him for his attempt, later, to re-enter and adorn more respectable and cultivated society. He was *not* a drinker to any extent, nor had he any business capacity, which latter fact explains his ultimate financial embarrassments, and his sad ending. He was the steward of exceptional talents."

More than a century ago an ancestor of Adam L. Gordon, a shrewd, industrious Scotch merchant of Bordeaux and Boulogne, laid the foundations of a house which reached a disastrous culmination on Friday, June 24, 1870, when a rising poet, and the most popular steeplechase rider in Australia, committed suicide in the scrub on Brighton Beach, Victoria. The merchant before-mentioned, a Mr. Robert Gordon, purchased the Barony of Esselmont, and settled himself at Worcester to enjoy a well-earned repose. Various professions were marked out for, or chosen by, his sons. One in particular, Adam D. Gordon, chose the army, and he served his country with distinction in the Indies. In 1825 he returned to England, and married

his cousin, Miss Harriet Gordon, who brought
with her a dowry of about £20,000. He returned to India, and was soon promoted to the
captaincy of a regiment of cavalry. He quickly
gained the love and admiration of the men for his
daring horsemanship and courageous conduct.
The exhaustiveness of the service ultimately broke
down his constitution, and he was compelled to
search for the repairing influences of a congenial
climate. During his wanderings he resided some
time at Fayal, in the Azores, where, in the year
1833, his only son, Adam Lindsay Gordon, was
born. Great and lasting was the affection that
existed between the daring father and the afterwards equally daring son, who in later years
would fondly recall with faltering voice his
father's affectionate care, and recount with
gleaming eye and animated gesture his father's
deeds in India. Writing in 1868, he said,
"There may be men living in India at
this moment who remember a certain officer
of irregular cavalry: this man, furnished with
a common boar spear and a sharp sabre, but
with no firearms, and mounted on his favourite
horse (probably not a pure Arab, but one of the
purest of that breed that could be obtained in
Hindostan), used to kill tigers single-handed on
open ground." Again, in "Whisperings in Wattle
Boughs," he says:

Oh, tell me, father mine, ere the good ship cross'd the
   brine,
  On the gangway one mute hand-grip we exchang'd ;
Do you, past the grave, employ, for your stubborn, reckless
   boy,
  Those petitions that in life were ne'er estrang'd ? "

In one of his letters, quoted by Mr. Sutherland,
the proud father thus describes the future poet :
" A sweet little fellow he is—indeed, I think almost
too pretty. Very slight and upright, carrying his
little curly head well back, and always swaggering
along. He talks with a sweet, full, laughing voice,
and face dimpled and bright as the morning. He
is seen here, perhaps, to .too great advantage in
any light clothing, scamping around the large play-
room."

As soon as Captain Gordon's health permitted
he returned to England, and ere long accepted
the position of Professor of Hindustani at Cheltenham College, where his son Lindsay received the
rudiments of his education. Here the lad remained for a few years, developing his taste for
horsemanship, and becoming noted among his
schoolfellows for his facility of rhyming verse,
some of which were descriptive of schoolboy
sports, others satirical sketches of obnoxious
teachers. Many wild escapades have been attributed to Gordon in his youth, and doubtless

upon good grounds. His name was erased from
the list of pupils at Cheltenham, for insubordi-
nation and other acts as culpable. He himself
admitted that he was expelled from another public
school for absenting himself in order to ride in a
steeplechase. It would almost be impossible for
an impressionable and enthusiastic youth like
Gordon to have been the companion of jockeys,
horse-trainers, livery stables keepers, and prize-
fighters without being, sooner or later, drawn
into the vortex of a life so full of temptation and
danger. His most notorious escapade—that in
connection with Black Tom Oliver—has often
been told, but the correct version of the story (as
near as it can possibly be ascertained) may be
worthy of repetition. Gordon, when a youth of
about seventeen, was anxious to distinguish himself at the Worcestershire Steeplechases, but he
was so well known, even then, as a reckless rider,
that he found it impossible to obtain a mount. In
despair he paid a man named Walker £5 for the
privilege of riding his mare next day at the races.
The same night it was seized by the Sheriff for a
debt owed by Walker, and locked up in the stables
of a Worcester hotel. Gordon failed to see the
justice of this, and, deeming that he had a certain
claim on the animal, broke into the stable and
took it away. He appeared at the races on the

following day, and, it is asserted, won the steeplechase in which he rode. But at the conclusion of
the race the officers of the law appeared, and
rescued the horse from its proud rider. He
escaped in the crowd, but a warrant was issued
for his arrest. The friendly intervention of Tom
Oliver, of Prestbury, and the payment of a monetary consideration by Captain Gordon, prevented
the execution of the warrant.

Of Gordon's school life little is known beyond
the fact that he was an apt, though somewhat
unruly, pupil, beloved by his schoolfellows for his
generous defence and assistance of the weak and
wanting. It was during these school years that
he developed his taste for poetry and classic
literature. One intimate friend of his in later
years declares that " no man formed his tastes for
literature so completely upon classical models,
though certainly one would not gather this from
his writings." Gordon once informed this friend
that he had never been able to learn much Greek
at school, and the most of what he had read was
since he had been in the bush. Despite this self-
depreciation it is worthy of note that he kept
terms at Merton College, Oxford, and " acquired
an elegant scholarship." He was very partial,
as may be easily believed, to the stirring verse of
Homer, as well as Virgil, Ovid, and Horace. He

invariably carried a Latin classic in his pocket, and so good a use did he make of it that it soon got into a sadly dilapidated condition. This would often occur with borrowed works, and when, with a rueful countenance, he would return the book to its owner, he would say "that he felt like one apologizing for knocking up a borrowed horse by over-riding."

After the Worcester Races' escapade it became more difficult than ever for the high-spirited youth to conform to the conventionalities demanded of him in the society in which he was privileged to move. At last, so unbearable had the restraint become, he resolved to leave his native country. This was in 1853, when the marvellous stories of the new El Dorados of Australia thrilled the Old World with almost unprecedented excitement, and with impatience at the old ways of getting rich. Gordon was urged to choose South Australia as the land of his adoption, on account of the letters of introduction to influential men with which his friends could furnish him. Three days before he sailed he wrote the pathetic verses, "To my Sister." They were addressed to Inez, his youngest sister, and were found among his papers, long after his death, by his friend and benefactor, Mr. John Riddock, of Yallum, S.A.

Gordon left England on the 7th of August, 1853,

bidding an affectionate farewell to his loving and beloved father on the deck of the ship *Julia*. With the independence of spirit which characterized all his actions through life, Gordon made little or no use of his letters of introduction, and soon after his arrival in South Australia joined the mounted police. The free life,

> " The vigour with which the air is rife !
> The spirit of joyous motion,"

the good horse, the dangerous episodes—all lent a charm to the trooper's occupation, and proved too tempting to the young man to resist, even had he felt a disposition to avoid them. Many were the adventures, dangers, and hardships he experienced in the wild life of an Australian trooper. Some of his experiences he embodied in verse, notably " Wolf and Hound," and " From the Wreck." The latter was founded upon an episode in connection with the wreck of the steamship *Admella*, which was driven ashore on the rocky coast of South Australia, near Cape Northumberland, one stormy night in August, 1859. The locality being very lonely and rarely visited, the crew and passengers were washed away before their terrible danger was discovered. Directly the calamity became known Gordon was despatched with the news to Mount

Gambier, and, according to the poem, killed his horse in the race with time. It may be here noted that the poem as originally published concluded with the following stanza, containing a pleasing reference to a brother poet :

> " There are songs yet unsung, there are tales yet untold
>   Concerning yon wreck that must baffle my pen ;
>   Let Kendall write legends in letters of gold,
>   Of deeds done and known among children of men."

" The Sick Stockrider " was also doubtless an Australian experience, and originally ended with the following lines :

> " I don't suppose I shall, though, for I feel like sleeping
>   sound ;
>   That sleep, they say, is doubtful. True ; but yet
>   At least it makes no difference to the dead man under
>   ground
>   What the living men remember or forget.
>   Enigmas that perplex us in the world's unequal strife,
>   The future may ignore or may reveal,
>   *Yet* SOME, *as weak as water, Ned ! to make the best of life,*
>   Have been, TO FACE THE WORST, AS TRUE AS STEEL."

These lines were sent to the editor of " Australian Poets "[1] by Mr. G. G. McCrae, who wrote : " I send you a verse I got from my friend John

---

[1] Griffith, Farran, Okeden, and Welsh.

Shillinglaw, who, like myself, was a friend of Gordon. I cannot conceive why Gordon should have cut out this concluding verse, as it seems to my mind to confer a completeness upon the whole that would be wanting without."

Gordon was also engaged on the South Australian Gold Escort in days full of wild and hazardous adventure, when men's lives often depended on the swiftness of their horses or the perfect condition of their firearms. It has been related of the poet, that once during his trooper career he had been instructed to take a lunatic to the nearest asylum, and was obliged to mount him on a half-broken horse. They jogged along happily enough all day, side by side, and at night lay down on the grass, handcuffed to one another. One night the madman was so restless that Gordon could get no sleep till he used the threat of a severe thrashing. This produced quietness, but next day Gordon imprudently suffered his prisoner to mount his trooper's horse with the pistols in the holsters, while he himself undertook to manage the more vicious animal. The tables were now turned, and the madman coolly drew the pistols and fired a well-directed but ineffectual shot before he was overpowered. During these trooper days Gordon made the acquaintance, in a rather peculiar fashion, of a boy who became famous as one of Australia's

best jockeys, "Tommy" Hales. This was while
the poet was at Penola. "Tommy" was about
ten or eleven years old, and in one of his mis-
chievous moods had brought down upon himself
the strong arm of the law, the result being that
he was conveyed to the lock-up for safety. Gordon heard of the affair, and doubtless remember-
ing his own wild doings on the Cotswold Hills,
and full of sympathy for boyish exuberance, re-
leased the repentant "Tommy." Long after, the
then two famous horsemen met at Lake Hawdon
Station, where Gordon was breaking in some young
colts, and spent many happy weeks together.

Gordon soon found that a trooper's life had
many unpleasant and disagreeable duties. These
he declined to perform, and ultimately left the
force in high dudgeon, because he had been called
upon to " shine " the boots of his superior officer.
He then became a horse-breaker, a business
specially dangerous to him on account of his
short-sightedness—a defect which exposed him to
ridiculous, as well as painful, accidents. On one
occasion he made an attempt to leap over a rail to
which horses were tethered at the Penola Hotel;
but as he was peering over the horse's head to
look for the rail the animal jumped clear from
under him. Frequently, in his wild gallops
through the bush, he was knocked out of his

saddle by the branches of trees, and sometimes was even rendered unconscious by the force of the collision. About the first horse-breaking engagement he had was at the station where he and "Tommy" Hales met after a long absence—Lake Hawdon, on Guichen Bay, owned by Mr. Stockdale. It was while in Mr. Stockdale's employ that Gordon made the acquaintance of the Rev. E. T. Woods, a large-hearted, sympathetic, and genial minister, with whom Gordon became very friendly. Mr. Woods was deeply impressed by the extraordinary character and superiority of the externally rough horse-breaker, and by his wide knowledge of classical Greek, Latin, French, and English authors, and thus describes his introduction to the future poet:

"My introduction to him was at a cattle station, Lake Hawdon, near Guichen Bay. He was breaking in a few horses for Mr. Stockdale, the proprietor. I arrived at the station in the evening, and he was at work, I remember, in the stockyard, sitting a young colt which was making surprising efforts to throw him. I watched the struggle for some minutes, and it ended by the girths breaking, and Gordon landed on his feet. We met that evening at supper, for in those days master and man, stranger and guest, all sat at the same table and shared the same fare. I remember little about Gordon that evening except that he was painfully near-sighted. He scarcely spoke. After supper he came to me upon the verandah and chatted for an hour; and I was surprised to find that his conversation was not about the usual station topics, but about poetry and poets. I was much interested, and inquired who he was as he went away. Mr. Stockdale could not tell me much. All he knew was that he was a good, steady lad and a splendid rider. He had been a mounted trooper when he came to the district, but after serving a short time had resigned, and taken to the employment in which I found him engaged. Mr. Stockdale further remarked that there was something above the common in Gordon. He never drank or gambled—two ordinary qualifications of bush hands in those days. He was not exactly a favourite, because he was rather moody and silent, and did not associate much with the men working with him, but, being quiet and obliging, was liked.

" Next morning he overtook me as I rode on my journey. His horse was a colt, half broken in, so that at first we could not converse much. He was going the same road as I was, to a station about forty miles away. As the day wore on, his horse settled down to his work, and we jogged along together.

" It is more than six-and-twenty years ago, yet
I can recall how much I was impressed with my
companion's knowledge, memory, and literary
tastes.   I thought him a most extraordinary
young man, and wished to see more of him.   He
had an odd way of reciting poetry, and his delivery
was monotonous, but his way of emphasizing the
beautiful portions of what he recited was charming
from its earnestness.   It was a puzzle to me then,
and still is, how he could manage to get books,
and how carry them about or get time to read
them.   His only leisure would be in the evening,
and then the light was generally a panican lamp
—that is, a honeysuckle cone stuck in clay in a
panican, and surrounded with mutton fat.   I have
a lively recollection of the difficulties I have had
myself in trying to read by such a lamp, and as
Gordon was so near-sighted I did not know how
he managed."

" In all his ways he was singular," says Mr.
Sutherland, " and his favourite manner of com-
posing is a matter of tradition in the neighbourhood.   When the bell rang for meals he was
rarely at hand, but could generally be discovered
high among the gnarled arms of a certain old gum
tree, where he loved to sit and smoke his favourite
' old black pipe,' known to readers of his verses.
There he would either croon over the poems of

greater authors than himself or compose his
own."

Mr. Woods found the horse-breaker to be pas-
sionately fond of poetry, and delighted at having
an opportunity of reciting his favourite passages
to sympathetic ears. But Gordon's elocution was
defective—one friend declaring that the poet's
recitations would make him laugh outright, they
were so " sing-song " and monotonous. Mr.
Woods relates an incident that illustrates the
whimsicalities of the poet. The two men were
overtaken in a storm on their way to Mount Gambier. The rain poured down in thorough Australian fashion. Night came on, the track was lost,
and the miserable travellers had no alternative
but to crawl under a tree, hungry and cold, and
wait the rising of the moon. Gordon, to beguile
the time, recited long passages from various
authors on the subject of storms, and concluded
his strange entertainment by reciting the whole
of the tempest scene from " King Lear." When
they reached a station the poet would not go to
bed, but walked about the supper-room reciting
" Childe Harold " till nearly morning. Gordon
was not very conversational, but when he did
converse there was, during his early years in
Australia, little of that sad, melancholy tone of
disappointment and fatalism so noticeable in some

of his poems. Nor was his conversation "horsey,"
nor his ways the ways of "horsey" men. A good
insight of his character is given by the rev. gentleman already quoted :

" In recalling these old memories about Gordon,
I can scarcely help asking myself the question,
why he was not received into whatever little
society there was in the bush in those days ?
Many men much his inferior in every way used
to be asked to the squatters' table, while except in
a few—a very few—places, my poet friend would
be sent to the men's hut, where there was one.
I am sure the fault did not lie so much with the
squatters as with himself. He was, as I say, very
shy and retiring. Very few knew that he was an
educated man and a gentleman. The fact is, that
he did not give them an opportunity. Often and
often I have heard the complaint made that Gordon would ride past the station without a glance
to the right or left, and perhaps camp in the
evening by himself a mile or so away. Many a
time, when I have seen his tall, gaunt figure
jogging past some station where I was staying,
have I ridden after him to try to bring him back,
or else to accompany him along the road. I was
seldom able to make him remain, but he was
always willing to have a companion at his camp ;
but I never heard him complain of this kind of

life.   He used to say it suited him, and sometimes compared the lot of a bushman with that of other states of mankind, saying that it was in many ways preferable to every one.

" At race times he generally rode where light weights were not required.   We had at all these meetings—and there was one every year for each township—an event called the Ladies' Purse. This was a bag of fancy work, containing a very extensive and valuable assortment of articles, which the ladies of the district used to make up. It included all kinds of fancy work and embroidery, such as smoking caps, slippers, belts, purses, &c. Only gentlemen riders could contend for it, and these must be accepted by a ladies' committee formed of those who had worked for the bag. Gordon applied for permission to ride for this prize at one meeting, and was refused.   He was much insulted at the refusal, but I don't think he said a word on the subject except to myself, and what he did say was very characteristic of the man.   He remarked that I used to blame him for not mixing more with the people of the district, and said ironically that this would show what little he would gain by consorting with such society.   It happened, moreover, that the coveted prize fell that year to the son of a squatter, who, a few years previously, had been a publican.   It was quite a disappointment to the ladies' committee, who expected the bag to fall into the hands of one who was better known and much more admired. They gave a practical effect to their dissatisfaction by taking the most valuable things out of the bag before it was given to the winner. This Gordon knew, and his comments upon it were very cynical."

It was true he was somewhat reckless, and was ever ready to try the most difficult jump—in fact, the more difficult it was the more pleasure he derived from it. Riding was his passion, and may be illustrated by a characteristic anecdote. On one occasion he lent one of his friends a horse—a good one, too—and on leaving him, said : " You can keep him, my boy, but be careful with him." The friend promised. Shortly after, Gordon returned and said : " Promise me one thing—one thing." "What is it ?" asked the friend, thinking some special instruction as to carefulness was to be given. " Let him take his fences *at his own pace*," was the reply. During his residence in the South-Eastern District Gordon earned for himself universal respect for his ability as a horseman and for his kindheartedness and generosity. In fact, the generosity of his nature became too widely known, and all manner of villainous horse-dealers and ostlers imposed upon him. Later on he tried

livery stable keeping at Narracoorte, but his tem-
perament unfitted him for the peculiar transac-
tions and the close attention to monetary matters
necessary to the achievement of success in that
otherwise congenial employment.

In 1862, in one of his reckless riding exploits,
he met with a severe accident, from the effects of
which he never completely recovered, but it was an
accident that had a great influence upon his after
life, for it was the means of introducing him to his
future wife—a Miss Park, who attended on him
while he was lying dangerously ill at the hotel in
Robe, which he was wont to frequent when in the
district. Gordon was greatly impressed with the
gentle ways of the girl, and above all with her
boldness on horseback. As soon as he was able
to get into the "pigskin" again he determined
that he would ask the girl to be his wife, and he
did so somewhat in this fashion: "Well, girl, I
like your ways. You seem industrious and sensible. If you like I will take a cottage at Robe,
and we will get married next week, and you shall
keep home for me." The girl consented. A week
later two horses were mounted, and the loving
couple rode eighty miles to Mount Gambier, where
they were married by the Rev. Mr. Don. The poet's
courtship was brief, and his marriage somewhat
hasty, but it was not therefore a case of " marry

in haste and repent at leisure." He loved his little, thrifty, girlish wife, and he was never tired of praising the devotion and courage which she manifested during his dark days of adversity. Years after the marriage he wrote: "She has more pluck in her little finger than I have in my whole body. Through all the worst of our troubles she bore up with wonderful spirit, and always cheered me and kept me straight." The home of the happy couple was picturesquely situated on a grassy slope overlooking the glorious sea, which he—like his brother poet, Kendall—loved so well. Many an hour he spent in solitary meditation by the seashore, and who shall tell the "long, long thoughts" of the brave-hearted, gentle poet as he looked out across the pulsating ocean beating between the loved land of his adoption and his manhood and the dear old home of his ancestors and his childhood! Doubtless he sang from his heart—

"I would that with sleepy soft embraces
    The sea would fold me—would find me rest
In luminous shades of her secret places,
    In depths where her marvels are manifest;
So the earth beneath her should not discover
My hidden couch—nor the heaven above her—
As a strong love shielding a weary lover
    I would have her shield me with shining breast.'

And yet some of his ballads, as an able journalist truly says, are pervaded by such a dashing, manly spirit and mental robustness that it seems difficult to identify the writer with any weak or morbid development. On the other hand, they also bear traces of sadness, almost approaching to despair, which it is now impossible to confound with those imaginary woes in the delineation of which poets are wont to find a pensive enjoyment. What might otherwise be regarded as merely the passing shadows of those sad hours which come to all of us some time or other, will now probably be viewed as the involuntary records of some real grief, the existence of which was never suspected even by poor Gordon's most familiar associates.

His home by the sea was neatly but plainly furnished, much in the then prevailing fashion of the Australian pioneer, with the exception, however, that on some simple bookshelves might have been seen works rarely to be met in the homes of early Australian colonists, such as Horace, Virgil, and Ovid. Horace's " De Arte Poetica " was a great favourite, and the passage, " *Si vis mi flere, dolendum est primum ipsi tibi* " he very frequently quoted.

In an article contributed to the *Adelaide Observer*, the late Mrs. N. A. Lord gave some interesting reminiscences of Gordon's life at Mount Gambier.

"Visiting, in that district, some people who knew the poet, the question was asked : 'Are there any friends of Gordon here?' The reply was : 'Gordon? Ah, poor fellow! Yes, I knew him. What a pity it was! He lived for some time about two miles out. He had a stable built adjoining his house, and a door led from his sitting-room into it—curious fancy of his. Did you ever see " Ingleside "? Beautiful creature. How is it he describes a racehorse ?'

> "'. . . Iron sinewed and satin skinned,
>   Ribbed like a drum, and limbed like a deer,
>   Fierce as the fire, and fleet as the wind,
>   There was nothing she couldn't climb or clear.'"

"'Gordon did not make many friends. He had an idea he had irretrievably lost caste. You know he was for some time in the police force, and had passed through many vicissitudes as to position ; he was convinced he could never again work into his old groove. A mistake! A gentleman every inch of him, and such a well-read fellow. He used to go to the parsonage here. Our parson was a man of large sympathies, and a capital classical scholar. I went up one evening and he and Gordon were spouting Greek and Latin, yards of it, and going into raptures over the old yarns—

Orpheus and his troubles, Galatea, and all the rest
of them.'

"I asked if Gordon wrote much of his poetry
while here.

"'He lived for some time down on the coast
near Cape Northumberland, and there most of the
poems in " Sea Spray and Smoke Drift " and some
of the " Bush Ballads " were written. I forget the
name of the place. That lady sitting by the fire
knew him well. Would you like to be presented ? '
Mine host made my name acceptable to the ' lady
by the fire,' and we were soon in close confab. I
told her of my wish to hear all I could of Gordon,
and she, being thoroughly ' simpatica,' said she
would tell me all she knew.

"'You ought to drive down and see Dingley Dell.
It was there, or rather on the wild seacoast close
by, with the roar of the Southern Ocean in his
ears, that so many of his poems were written. Do
you know " The Swimmer " and " From the
Wreck"? In these you will find an exact description of the scenery by which he was surrounded.'

" In the course of our converse I came upon the
following : ' Mr. Gordon used often to come to
my father's house, and we exchanged confidences
on the subject of the " Idylls of the King," Law-
rence's and Whyte Melville's novels. " Barren
Honour" was a great favourite of his ; he liked

Browning, too, and would repeat long pieces from any poem he admired in a strange, deep monotonous voice, and with such a fire burning in his dark, cavernous eyes. He often rode his grey mare " Modesty " to our house, and one day as he was leaving I timidly remarked that I had enjoyed seeing her fly over the jumps at a late steeple-chase. He replied, while. arranging the mare's headpiece, and without looking at me (he very seldom raised his eyes to my face)—' You should see Ingleside,' he said. ' I am training him now. Going to ride him next week at C——. I take him in and out of the Lake paddocks every morning.' "

" ' Could " Modesty " jump that fence? ' I asked, indicating a stiff one just outside our garden. He assented eagerly, and after saying farewell he took the grey over four of the fences within view of our drawing-room windows, to my mother's dismay and my great delight.'

" I then asked her if she further superintended the training of ' Ingleside.'

" ' Could I resist it ? Three mornings that next week found me, raceglass in hand, watching the splendid horse and his utterly fearless rider, over some very stiff timber. Mr. Gordon used to ride up to where I sat on a fallen tree, and we would talk horses or poetry for a few minutes, never longer.

" ' The third time I walked past the Blue Lake and down to the Flat beyond, after the usual performance, the horse and rider came up for a word of praise. As I was turning to go home, to my astonishment Mr. Gordon said, his eyes fixed on the landscape ahead—

" ' Does your mother know you come to see me jump ? '

" I must confess to having been entirely disconcerted, but I told him the unvarnished truth. ' No, she would be horrified.   She thinks racing wicked, and could not look at a horse jumping.'

" ' Good-bye,' he said.   ' Don't come again.'

" This was a new experience to me.   Hitherto, if you will not mind my saying so, I had been accustomed to view the act of repression from the active, not the passive side. I dare say the change was wholesome, but not pleasant. I took my hand from my muff and offered it in farewell. He looked at it as if it were some natural curiosity.

" ' It is the first time I have touched a lady's hand for many a day—my own fault—my own fault—good-bye ; you don't know the world.   I do ; don't come again.' He spoke in his usual strange monotone, and before I had time to think or speak he was on the grey and away. As I walked home the country looked strangely misty. Mr. Gordon always seemed so sad, hopelessly sad, and you can see a vein of despairing sorrow in almost all his poems. As to his advice, I am sure he was right, but I was young then, and girls do not fear Mrs. Grundy.' "

The following morning a visit was made to Dingley Dell (where Gordon had lived) by way of Port MacDonnell, a small town under the lee of Cape Northumberland.

Mrs. Lord thus describes the visit :

" Leaving the coast, when about half a mile from a rocky headland whereon is planted a noble lighthouse, we struck inland and were soon passing through a dense grove of wattles just bursting into bloom, box shrubs which were not yet clothed with their creamy-white plumes (so like the English meadowsweet), and another tall shrub which the boy called teatree, but is not the tree usually known by that name, and here at once I recognized the sights and sounds which Gordon so constantly described. We were startled as we passed under a grim-looking dead white-gum by an unearthly din overhead—

> " ' Harshly break those peals of laughter
>   From the jays aloft.'

And a little further on—

> " ' Hark ! the bells on distant cattle
>   Waft across the range

> Through the golden-tufted wattle
>   Music, low and strange ! '

As if to follow the poet word for word, we—

> " ' . . . Round the black teatree belt
>   Wheeled to the west,
>   We crossed a low range, sickly
>   Scented with musk
>   From wattle-tree blossom. We
>   Skirted a marsh,
>   *   *   *   *
>   And pealed overhead the jay's
>   Laughter note harsh.'

Again, as we passed through a grove of tall wattles,
brilliantly green grass beneath, a speckless sky
above, I am reminded of his words in ' By Wood
and Wold '—

> " ' 'Tis pleasant, I ween, with a leafy screen
>   O'er the weary head, to lie
> On the mossy carpet of emerald green,
>   'Neath the vault of the azure sky.'

" We passed along the range, now through
dense bowers, then across open glades, anon
beneath giant white gum-trees, whose dreary
fantastic age Gordon so well describes—

> " ' On slopes of the range.
> Where the gnarl'd, knotted trunks eucalyptian
> Seem carved, like weird columns Egyptian,
> With curious device, quaint inscription,
>   And hieroglyph strange.'

"At last we emerged on a bush road, at one side of which a brush fence guarded a pleasant-looking homestead—a white-walled cottage with its side to the road, and facing what (if the building had been more pretentious) we should have called a wide, well-kept lawn, vividly green, surrounded by knolls, on which were groves of wattles, and here and there the beautiful flowering gum, a small tree, or tall shrub, which I believe is rare. It has three distinct varieties—creamy-white, deep crimson, and pale pink, the blossom being about three times the size of the ordinary gum flower.

" ' There, sir,' said the boy, ' that is Dingley Dell.'

" Yes, there was the roof which had sheltered the active form, the restless brain of the poet ; from here he used to wander afoot through the pretty dells or on the range, whence, through and over a waving sea of treetops, the blue Southern Ocean flashes in the distance, or, on one of his good steeds, scouring beaten tracks, gates, and slip-panels, across country to Allandale and Mount Gambier ; but very often his steps turned to the coast, and there some of his best lines were roughly jotted down. There are, I fancy, few Australians, at all events few Victorians, who do not know ' Visions in the Smoke.' The first stanza points to the life, the scene which met our eyes when, with many lingering looks backward cast at Dingley Dell, we followed our young guide up the steep road, and at last came in view of the sea.

> " ' Rest, and be thankful !   On the verge
>   Of the tall cliff, rugged and grey,
>   At whose granite base the breakers surge,
>   And shiver their frothy spray,
>   Outstretched, I gaze on the eddying wreath
>   That gathers and flits away,
>   With the surf beneath, and between my teeth
>   The stem of the " ancient clay."
>   *   *   *   *
>   The neutral tint of the sullen sea
>   Is flecked with snowy foam,
>   And the distant gale sighs drearilie,
>   As the wanderer sighs for his home ;
>   The white sea-horses toss their manes
>   On the bar of the southern reef,
>   And the breakers moan, and (by Jove, it rains !)
>   I thought I should come to grief.'

" I shall never forget the grandeur of the scene. The ' Hollow roar of the surf on the shore ' is a sound unknown to the dwellers by the quiet waters of Hobson's Bay. ' A dull discordant monotone ' which brings to one's inner consciousness a dim but painful sense of impending trouble ; and with what gigantic force come in the great rollers ! Here we experience the grand unbroken swell of the Southern Ocean; no obstacle, no break between us and the South Pole! The 'Song of the Surf' is a word-picture of what lies before us:

" ' White steeds of ocean, that leap with a hollow and wearisome roar
On the bar of ironstone steep, not a fathom's length from the shore.'

" Surely Gordon must have stood on this spot when he wrote that unhappy ' Quare Fatigasti':

" ' Two years ago I was thinking
On the changes that years bring forth ;
Now I stand where I then stood, drinking
The gust and the salt sea froth ;
And the shuddering wave strikes, linking
With the wave subsiding, sinking,
And clots the coast herbage, shrinking,
With the hue of the white cere-cloth.'

" In ' The Swimmer ' I found, as the ' lady by the fire' predicted, still clearer word-painting of what meets my eyes :

" ' Rocks receding, and reefs flung forward.

A grim, grey coast, with a seaboard ghastly,
And shores trod seldom by foot of men,
Where the battered hull and the broken mast lie—
They have lain embedded these long years ten.' "

In 1864 Gordon received, much to his satisfaction—for it relieved pressing monetary claims and opened up a vista of leisure and study—a considerable sum of money, amounting, it is believed, to about £7,000. This money he inherited at his father's death, which occurred in 1857. It is very probable that the poet would never have received the money, nor heard of his father's death, but for the perseverance and good offices of Sir A. Trotter, one of the trustees. The receipt of the money set him thinking upon the advisableness of a trip "home"—an ambition of all true Australians ere they die; but he disliked the idea of leaving the colonies, the friends he had made, and the associations he had formed. He once asserted that he had become too rough and uncouth for the civilization of Europe, and expressed the utmost horror at being surrounded by the trammels, and oppressed with the shams, of a so-called polite society. In this same year Gordon published at Mount Gambier a poem entitled "The Feud." It treated the same subject as the "Braes of Yarrow," written by Hamilton. The following stanza from the poem has been quoted as illustrating the author's "strong individuality" and "usual fire."

"His next-of-kin by blood and birth
May claim his horses and land,

> The groom may black his saddle girth
>   And bid his charger stand,
> But never a man on God's wide earth
>   Shall touch his darling's hand."

Gordon's horsemanship and poetical talents had now become well known throughout the district of Victoria, S.A., where he resided, and where he held landed property. His receipt of a legacy added to the respect in which he was held, and folk began to look up to him as a country gentleman. About this time the electors of the district became dissatisfied with one of their representatives, Attorney-General R. I. Stow, who was considered to be giving too much support to the squatters. The electors wished to be represented by a local man who could go to Adelaide and give proper attention to their interests. Adam L. Gordon being regarded as a "fit and proper person," he was solicited to offer himself as a candidate. But he did not favour the idea, declaring his unsuitableness for the responsible office of legislator, owing to his being a poor speaker, and having but little acquaintance with the pressing questions of the day. Mr. Woods claims to have been influential in obtaining Gordon's determination to accept the nomination. He says:

"As fresh instances were made, he consulted

me on the subject, and I prevailed upon him to
accept the position. I must say that my advice
was mainly for his own sake. I thought it would
give him occupation, which he evidently needed,
and might open to him a successful, if not a
brilliant career. I must own, too, that he had
shown a tendency to a morbid melancholy about
which I was not without apprehensions. He used
to complain a good deal that he was not in any
useful career; that his life was being wasted,
and so forth, and he indulged more and more his
solitary habits, walking and riding alone, or sitting
for hours by the seaside. I was very glad, therefore, to see him plunge into the excitement of a
contested election."

On January 11, 1865, he was presented with a
"respectably signed" requisition, and, after a little
hesitation allowed himself to be put in nomination for the district. On the afternoon of the same
day he attended a meeting of the electors held at
Long's Assembly Rooms, Mount Gambier. This
meeting had been called by the Returning Officer
to hear the views and opinions of candidates.
Gordon was introduced to the meeting by Mr.
Burton, and made the following speech. He said,
"It appeared from the requisition that he had
received, that some of them desired that he should
come forward as a candidate for the representation

of the district in the next Parliament. He had received the requisition but that morning, and he did not wish to say much on the subject as yet. He knew it was usual for aspirants for Parliamentary honours to make grand addresses to the public on such occasions—to grow eloquent on their wrongs, and the abuses of the past and present Governments. When a boy he had been amused to listen to such men. They promised a great deal. They were about to rectify the evils that had crept into the affairs of the present world, and he was not sure but they held out vague hopes of reforming the next. But these men most frequently promised one way and performed another. These men, like the celebrated character of a celebrated writer, told their constituents that they could call spirits from the deep; but they forgot the very natural query which followed the boast—' Will they come when they are called ?' He could do as they did, no doubt ; but he had no intention of doing so. He would promise as little as possible. He did not know that he had any special adaptedness for being their representative. They would get many more better fitted than himself, and he did not desire to thrust himself upon them. If they could get a better man he would gladly give way to him ; and he would not feel annoyed in the event of a contest at their voting for another. He did not wish, however, to treat them too cavalierly. If they did return him as their member, they would find him grateful for the honour, and that their confidence in him was not misplaced."

Gordon was subjected to the usual "heckling," which he resented with some spirit. In reply to one persistent elector, he said, "he thought Mr. P—— was jumping at conclusions. He seemed to forget that there was generally a diversity of opinion on most questions, and that very probably as many of the public would be opposed to his way of thinking as were in favour of it. It was hard to serve two masters, but it was a great deal harder to serve half-a-dozen. However, he did not seek Mr. P——'s support, and he certainly would not alter his opinions to bespeak the favour of any section of the community. He did not understand when he came to the meeting that he would be called upon to speak. He was not prepared to do so. It was only the other day that the idea of going to Parliament was suggested to him, and he was willing to bow to the majority whether he should go there or not."

On the following Wednesday (Jan. 18th) he addressed a meeting of the electors in the same room, Dr. Wehl occupying the chair. The candidate lost no time in giving a plain, straightforward,

and unhesitating explanation of his views and
opinions upon the topics of the day. Upon the
question of free distillation, he said " he thought
the Government wisely raised a large revenue from
spirits. It was a tax paid by the wealthy and
those who could well afford it. If the revenue
ever became so large that the country could dispense with any part of it, he should prefer to
lighten the taxes on the necessaries of life." He saw
very clearly the evils of the existing immigration
system, and declared that " unless the Government sanctioned a more equitable distribution of
the immigrants on their arrival in the colony, he
would oppose its continuance." On that burning
Australian question, fiscal reform, he had very
pronounced views. He said he " was in favour
of *ad valorem* duties. They were a most fair
way of raising a revenue." He wisely saw, so far
back as 1865, that one of the essentials of
Australian prosperity and solidarity was an
" assimilation of Australian tariffs," which he
strongly advocated. He was loudly cheered for
approving of the system of borrowing money for
reproductive public works. " Some people," said
he, " have a horror of a national debt. I have no
sympathy with them. So long as we have a
boundless country of undeveloped resources to
mortgage for the small sum that would be necessary

to push it ahead, we are acting on a wrong principle in being so cautious." He concluded this very interesting speech as follows : " It is proposed to bind the candidates neck and heels to do the bidding of the electors. I do not mean to submit to that process. I will go into Parliament free and independent, if at all. I will let you know my sentiments freely, but I reserve to myself the right to modify them, and not to please all the electors on this side of the Equator will I bind myself down not to do so. I will assure you, however, that I do not change my mind very readily, and am very conservative of my opinions."[1] There spoke Adam L. Gordon. In answer to questions, he declared himself in favour of " local self-government," opposed to the " opening of public-houses on the Sabbath," and not in favour of " doing away with the custom house and taking the land revenue for the ordinary purposes of Government."

The election resulted in Gordon defeating Attorney-General Stow by three votes. This election was an important one ; the defeat of Mr. Stow, who was the Attorney-General in the existing Ministry, and Leader in the House of Assembly, being followed by the resignation of

[1] This speech—Gordon's first hustings' address—is given in full on page 180.

the Ministry of Sir Henry Ayres. On May
23, 1865, "Mr. Gordon took the oath and
his seat for the Electoral District of Victoria."
On the 31st of the same month he delivered
his first Parliamentary speech. The question
before the House was the annual leases of
squatters. Gordon's speech was brief and to
the point. He told the House that "he was not
a squatter, and had no interest in squatting," but
he thought "there could be no advantage in
sacrificing the squatters, and no man could fail to
see the hardship that must accrue to many of
them if their runs were put up for auction as
proposed." On the 6th of June he returned to
the question, and delivered an interesting speech,
which is reproduced in full on page 191, from the
Hansard of the time, because it is so thoroughly
Gordonesque, and because lovers of the poet will
gladly welcome it as another illustration of his
vari-sided character. He was listened to with
patience and attention by a House that was
amused at his eccentricities and interested in the
aptness of his classical quotations. He attended
Parliament with regularity for some months, and
endeavoured to fulfil his promises to the electors.
He voted on nearly all questions that were placed
before the House, and took charge of numerous
petitions from his district. On June the 17th

he voted for a Bill to prevent the influx of West Australian criminals to South Australia. He took part in a no-confidence debate, and supported the Ministry of the day because he thought "they had not had a fair opportunity of stating their policy." In November of the same year he again made one of those semi-classical speeches with which he entertained the House. The subject was the appointment of Mr. H. E. Downer as Commissioner in Insolvency. A motion had been made disapproving the appointment. Gordon supported the Government, declaring that "he could not see the utility of such ceaseless strife, which tended to impede the progress of the business indefinitely. The Opposition were like the heads of the hydra—*Quique redundabat facundo vulnere serpens.*" The whole speech is given elsewhere.

During the time Parliament was in Session, Gordon was a frequent visitor to the Parliamentary library, the books that interested him most being —not Blue Books, Reports of Committees, or *Hansard*—but the ancient and modern classics. Of the latter he very much favoured Racine and Corneille. He had an intimate knowledge of French, but his pronunciation was defective, though once in his early years he had resided in France. He soon tired of politics, and it is reported of him that he spent much time drawing caricatures of the members and making sketches of horses. His abstinence from speech-making became so noticeable, that a sketch writer in one of the papers of the day said, " The talk is that the seconder was short, if he was not sweet ; that impertinent persons are asking how it is Mr. Gordon has never done anything since his first great classical, mythological, and 'oratorical oration ' (if Mr. Coglin will excuse us) ; that English history tells of a ' Single-speech Hamilton,' whose notoriety the member for Victoria should seek to avoid ; that at any rate it is better to say little, if it is good, than much, if it is bad." These remarks were made in consequence of his very brief speech in seconding the adoption of the address in reply to the Governor's opening speech. He confessed in those brief sentences that he " did not feel capable of speaking upon the policy of the country at. large, but he quite agreed that they wanted no taxation, except, perhaps, a tax on wire fencing." His appearances in the House gradually lessened, and at the General Election he did not put himself in nomination. Thus his career as a legislator ended (doubtless owing to pecuniary disabilities), and it simply lived in his recollection as a humorous episode in his strange career.

An eminent South Australian statesman of the old days, and still a very prominent and honoured figure in the affairs of his adopted land, informs me that he distinctly remembers Gordon when he sat in the South Australian Legislature. He was very clever with his pencil, continually making humorous sketches of Parliamentary incidents, enlivened with "tags of rhyme." His caricatures of political orators were full of harmless humour, and strikingly characteristic. So well known had this gift of his become, that it was a common thing to be saluted with the query, " Have you seen Gordon's picture of So-and-so ? " He had a " happy knack " of hitting off the facial peculiarities and the oratorical attitudes of speakers. " I well remember," says the statesman referred to, "one sketch he made. It was of an election meeting, giving portraits of the chairman and the candidate, the man who talked the most nonsense and the man who got the most drunk. This was one of his most successful efforts, and caused great mirth when it was exhibited, Gordon himself looking on as stolid as if he had in some way committed himself." His desk in the House was always surrounded by admiring friends, anxious to read his latest rhymes or see his most recent sketch. He was everybody's friend, and, despite his reserve, was always courteous and gentlemanly. Members frequently neglected the routine of the House for the sake of a "chat with Gordon." He himself was not much interested in politics, and simply endeavoured to do his duty to his constituents, whose interests had been sadly neglected. He was a regular visitor to the Parliamentary library, and was rarely without a classic in his pocket. This particular "Parliamentary privilege" he prized more than all the others put together. He was greatly missed after his resignation, and his absence was frequently bemoaned by those who had been amused by his wit and interested by his converse.

The gentleman who relates the above declares that the portrait which appears as a frontispiece to this volume is a remarkably good likeness, and should prove very acceptable to the poet's numerous admirers.

Gordon contributed to various newspapers at this time, the *Colonial Monthly* and *Bell's Life in Victoria* being among the number. The favourable reception of his contributions began to fill him with high hopes of success in literature, and, strange to say, like Kendall, this success strongly prompted him to visit the "Queen City of the South," as Victorians call their capital. But the turf and the hunt still maintained their charms for him. He loved—

" The spirit of joyous motion ;
The fever, the fulness of animal life,
   Can be drained from no earthly potion !
The lungs with the living gas grow light,
   And the limbs feel the strength of ten,
While the chest expands with its madd'ning might—
   God's glorious oxygen !"

And it is in his racing verses that this love finds such spontaneous and powerful expression. His description of the Melbourne Cup of 1867, won by Tim Whiffler, " stands perfectly unique as a specimen of what racing poetry should be. No poet has drawn a picture more true to nature."

In September, 1865, he rode Mr. J. C. James's " Cadger " in the Grand Annual Steeplechase of the South Australian Jockey Club, and won the race easily. In December of the same year his victories with his great steeplechaser, " Ballarat," made his name famous in Australian sporting circles, and he plunged deeper than ever into the whirlpool of racing, making sad havoc of the fortune that had been left to him.

It was while resident in South Australia that he made his famous jump with " Red Lancer," over the fence on the Port MacDonnell Road, between the Blue and Leg of Mutton Lakes of Mount Gambier. Reference has been made to this locality by " Bruni," a well-known contributor to the *Australasian*. He writes : " Immediately below is the pretty little Leg of Mutton Lake, with the cottage and nursery of the forester at one end, a low ridge separating it from the large valley lake, which extends to the far end of the great crater-like depression in which these lakes lie. At the western end of this basin the highest peak of the hill rises almost perpendicularly from the water's edge. Black volcanic rocks are seen all the way to the summit, with scarcely a trace of vegetation on the rugged surface. Following the metalled road about a quarter of a mile further, I reach the path trending to the right which leads to the summit of the Mount. It was near this spot that the late A. L. Gordon is said to have jumped his horse in and out of the fence that runs round the Blue Lake. The fence, though of a good height and strongly made, is one that any ordinary hunter could clear with ease, but the feat is rendered extremely dangerous owing to the small space on the lake side of the fence for a horse to land and take off again. The slightest mistake would have hurled horse and rider into the lake two hundred feet below. It is just such a thing as Gordon would have done in those days." The poet and some sporting friends from Victoria were riding in the neighbourhood, and the conversation turned on feats of horsemanship witnessed in the

vicinity. Gordon was immediately inflamed with
a desire to perform a feat that he felt sure none
of his friends would dare emulate. He carried
" Red Lancer" over the fence, and, by leaping
from rock to rock, cleared a chasm more than forty
feet wide, the noble horse seeming to be inspired
with the fearless courage of its rider. Among the
friends who were present was Mr. W. Trainor, of
Coleraine, a devoted admirer, companion, and correspondent of the poet. He had seen Gordon write
many of his poems with a stump of lead pencil on
the backs of envelopes, and has the distinction of
being the first to hear that popular poem, " The
Sick Stockrider," read by the author himself, on
the evening of the day on which it was written.
Mr. Trainor has declared to equal enthusiastic
admirers of the poet that Gordon was always a
quiet, modest, pure-minded gentleman, and that
he had never heard a bad word from his lips.
" You know," said Mr. Trainor to Mr. Thomas,
" how men talk in the bush. Gentlemen are often
as bad as bullock-drivers. Gordon wasn't like
that. I never knew such a noble-hearted man,
especially where women were concerned, and he
was the best horseman—well, he and James
Wilson were the best horsemen—I ever saw." Mr.
Thomas, in referring to Gordon's correspondence
with Mr. Trainor, says, " In all these letters one

perceives the striking modesty of the poet. When he describes how he 'forced the running' at a certain juncture, he says, 'Perhaps I was wrong in this, but I thought it best.' There is no note of self-laudation in any of his writings. That was his life."

About the close of 1865 Gordon possessed a considerable extent of land between Mount Gambier and Penola, which he occupied for pasturage purposes. He also owned land at Nickol Bay, in West Australia. Shortly after his retirement from Parliament his South Australian runs were subdivided and leased out as farms—an incident which doubtless inspired the poem " Exodus Parthenidæ ; or, The Lay of the Last Squatter," which is reprinted in this volume for the first time. The poem has no special merit, but as it is an interesting Australian picture, and a genuine " Gordon," it is hoped the lovers of the poet will appreciate its appearance. Gordon's small heritage gradually dwindled away under the pressure of racing demands and the " sharking " tendencies of turf friends, and he was compelled to part from his territorial possessions. With their realization he cleared off his accounts—for he scorned to owe any man anything. In November, 1867, he went to Ballarat, and, renting Craig's stables, opened a " livery and bait " business, having also charge

of the hounds of the Hunt Club. He and his
faithful wife struggled hard to succeed, but,
through his incapacity for business details, failure
seemed ever to dog his footsteps. Patronage was
extensive, business was brisk, but money was slow,
for people neglected to pay their accounts, and left
the unfortunate livery stable keeper to meet his
expenses out of his capital. About a month after
he had been in business, and just as he was
beginning to wonder how he would "make ends
meet," he received a small legacy bequeathed to
him by his father's first cousin. This enabled him
to satisfactorily settle his affairs, and leave an
occupation that was exceedingly distasteful to
him. He sold off his household furniture and
effects, and, as the hard work and worry had
affected Mrs. Gordon's health, he sent her back to
her father at Yallum, S.A., in order to recruit her
failing energies. She was glad to get away from
a place so full of sad associations, for beside the
business failure she had here lost a little daughter,
to whom she was devotedly attached. Gordon
took his wife to Melbourne, and, with a bitter
melancholy in his heart, waived his adieu to her
who had so patiently borne her share of his mis-
fortunes. He returned to Ballarat with the
shadow of melancholy deepened into the black-
ness of despair. Life was a burden to him, and

he longed to unravel the riddle. In the bitterness
of his soul he asks—

> " Is there aught worth losing or keeping?
>   The bitters or sweets men quaff?
>   The sowing or the doubtful reaping?
>   The harvest of grain or chaff?
>   Or squandering days or heaping,
>   Or waking seasons or sleeping,
>   The laughter that dries the weeping,
>   Or the weeping that drowns the laugh?"

Suicide seemed ever present to his mind.
Vainly he had sought " surcease of sorrow " in
the congenial employments of the past. No rest
came to his perturbed soul. Mr. Sutherland
quotes the following letter as indicative of his
state of mind at this period of his life :

"You have no idea how sick I am of steeplechasing and horse-riding, but when a man gets
so deep into the mire it is hard to draw back. . . .
I never got over that fall, and since then I have
taken to drink—at least, though I never get
drunk, I drink a great deal more than I ought to
do ; for I have a good deal of pain in my head
and neck, and I am sometimes so low-spirited and
miserable, that if I had a strong sleeping draught
near me I might take it. I have carried one that
I should never wake from, and if I could only
persuade myself that I am a little mad I might

do something of that sort. I really do feel a
little mad sometimes, and I begin to think I have
more trouble than I can endure ; I would almost
say more than I deserve, but this would probably
be untrue."

He longed to get away from the turf and its
associations. But he found it impossible. His
friends were chiefly of the turf, and he saw no
other way of earning a livelihood. At last he
accepted an engagement to attend to the stables
of a gentleman at Toorak. He also became a
well-known figure on the Victorian racecourses
and at the hunt meets. He gloried in a good
hunt, and was moved to wrath on one occasion
because a hunt, in which he had taken part,
had been, from his point of view, wrongly
described. He broke through his usual reserve
and sent the following very severe reply to the
paper in which the faulty report appeared :—

" SIR,—I read an account of the run with the
Melbourne hounds from the Essendon Pound in
your columns last week. I have not the least
idea who your correspondent, ' Actæon,' may be,
nor does it much matter. Perhaps he never saw
the run, and almost certainly he never saw the
best of it. At least, if by any chance he was in
the first flight, I can only say his version of

what took place is a most extraordinary one. If he was not there, he might have taken the trouble to make himself better acquainted with some of the facts. An account in some respects more utterly at variance with the truth I have seldom read, and this can be proved so easily, that I do not suppose he would care to reply in his own name as I do in mine.—A. L. GORDON."

His popularity as a rider was only equalled by his reputation for honesty. He rode to win, not, as he said once, "to suit the books." Sorely as he was tempted—very sorely for one in his comparatively indigent circumstances—he never succumbed. The "filthy lucre" for filthy work could go to others; to him the honour and glory of victory on his well-loved horse was all-sufficing, and one intimate friend writing of him (appropriately naming him "Reckless"), said, "My friend Reckless has ridden many steeple-chases, and won some of them, and is a man whom one might reasonably expect to have seen the folly of most things. But he has not. Riding is a passion with him, but betting is not. I am certain that Reckless would ride against Death on the pale horse if the grim old fellow would only give him six pounds and a bit of a start. Name a jump, and he was on fire to

ride at it.   Curtius and his famous gulf were
nothing to him."

" The other day I went out to ride with Reckless.   There were four of us in all.   Reckless had
brought two friends, both of whom were admirers
of his, and was prepared for any amount of
falls.   Both his friends were horsey—that is to
say, both of them were interested in horseflesh,
and each 'fancied himself' as a rider.   All the
way down to our destination Reckless was
taking timber, and it was with much difficulty
that we could dissuade him from attempting
something like 30ft. of fly over a stone-banked
gutter, with a strong four-rail at each side of
it.   I believe, indeed, that he would have gone at
it after all had we not all three agreed that the
jump was impossible for anything four-footed.   He
is usually rather wild in his ways, but on this
particular day he was wilder than ever.   He had
the misfortune to be mounted upon a 'little mare,'
and we all know what an encouragement to folly
that is.

" We were close to St. Kilda, where a broad
drain runs towards the sea, faced on each side
with bluestone, and with a high-sawn fence on
either side.   We were looking at this obstacle,
and I hazarded the remark, 'That's a yawner;
but I have seen horses in Leicestershire that

I believe would fly the lot.' Gordon was riding a little bay mare named 'Maude,' and the words were hardly out of my mouth when he wheeled the mare round, and trotted a few yards with the intention of having 'a go' at the drain; and it was all Marcus Clarke could do to induce him not to make the attempt. That he would have tried and have killed the mare, and have probably broken his own neck, I am convinced; and it was not until he had jumped nearly every fence about the park that he seemed to calm down."

Certain it was that no man could take every ounce out of a horse better than he could, and no man could tell a horse in more unmistakable language that a rider with an iron will and un-flinching determination was on his back. If he had a weakness it was for forcing the pace and picking out the biggest panel; and if he had a failing as a jockey it was at the finish of a race, when fine hands and artistic riding are often called into requisition. As instancing the fatalism that strongly marked his views of life, it may be noted here that he was always "last out" of the saddling paddock. On being questioned about this peculiarity he would only reply that he always made it a rule to be "last out" when he was going to ride a steeplechase. His manner of

sitting a horse over a big fence was unique, and
any one who had witnessed his peculiar habit
of throwing himself back in the saddle as the
horse surmounted the obstacle could never afterwards mistake him.   In riding to hounds he
loved a stiff country and big timber that would
test the cleverness of the horses and the pluck
of their riders. The Press of the day were as
unanimous as the public in their praise of his
prowess as a rider. When he appeared on the
course the people cried exultingly, "Here comes
Gordon!" "Gordon wins!" "Bravo, Adam!" &c.;
while the Press related how "Mr. Gordon rode in
his usual plucky style," or "Mr. Gordon looked as
quiet and as at home as he always looked—the
beau ideal of a gentleman rider," or "Mr. Gordon's
fine horsemanship deserves every praise." The
poet's most famous performance in steeplechasing occurred at the Melbourne Hunt Club
Meeting of October 10, 1868, when he won, on
the same day, the Hunt Club Cup on Major
Barker's "Babbler"; the Metropolitan Handicap
Steeplechase on his own horse "Viking," and the
Selling Steeplechase on his own horse "Cadger,"
the last-named being an old favourite with the
public. Gordon had thus ridden and won three
steeplechases without a fall—truly a great performance, and "certainly put," as the papers of

the day said, "a great feather in Mr. Gordon's cap."

There are writers who say that these races were ridden with a recklessness of danger that was simply intended to court death. Certainly the poet had many serious falls, that off " Prince Rupert," in November, 1869, being particularly severe ; but I incline to the belief that he loved the sport too well to seek his death by it. He did not love it as a money-making employment, but he loved it because he believed that—

> " . . . If once we efface the joys of the chase
>   From the land, and outroot the stud,
>   Good-bye to the Anglo-Saxon race !
>   Farewell to the Norman blood ! "

He would gladly have severed his connection with racing men, whom he once declared to be " Ishmaelites, their hands against every man's, and every man's against theirs." Of bookmakers and bookmaking he had plain and pronounced views. He once said, " A good bookmaker may be better than a bad clergyman, and we have good bookmakers amongst us. But there are men who wager openly, and do their business without let or hindrance, and whose disreputable practices bring discredit upon all whose profession may be in any respect identical or even similar. These are the carrion birds of the turf, who hover to and fro on the confines of the ring, seeking for the corpses upon which they may gorge themselves to repletion."

On another occasion he wrote : " If I stopped much longer at this sort of game, I should not be so particular as I ought to be. If I could find any sort of work that I could live by I would swear against ever going near a racecourse again. I am heartily tired of the life I have been leading, and have never enjoyed a ride since my fall, except a hunt, when Mrs. Gordon rode well alongside of me."

Towards the close of 1868, or the beginning of 1869, Mrs. Gordon joined her husband in Melbourne. Shortly after he took apartments at Brighton with a market gardener named Hugh Kelly. He now strove harder than ever to free himself from the trammels of the turf, but without avail. He could not earn a livelihood away from the turf, and was therefore compelled to eke out a bare subsistence by the training of horses and by occasionally contributing poetry and prose to the newspapers. In the latter occupation he was much assisted and encouraged by the good-heartedness of Mr. W. J. Hammersley, who relates how Gordon refused at first to accept money for his contributions, but was ultimately induced to alter his determination, as he was in very straitened circumstances. "He, in fact," says Mr. Hammersley, "told me as much, and I used to get him a cheque every now and then and slip it quietly into his hand with every regard for his feelings. For he was a very proud man, and, notwithstanding his bushman's attire and rough exterior, there was no mistaking the gentleman. It was in the yard of the Hunt Club Hotel, in Little Collins Street, that I once met him with Walter Montgomery, the actor, and the latter insisted on Gordon's riding about a little pony. Gordon's legs touched the ground, and he seemed to enjoy the joke immensely, especially as it pleased the actor. I understood from him that his father had been an officer in the army, that he was entitled to a considerable property at home, and that he would go to England to see after it. He once brought some law papers into my office, and referred to them as relating to the property to which he was entitled. He seemed terribly in earnest over them, and his eye, that wild eye, seemed to look into one's very soul as he conversed. At times he was the strangest, most weird, mysterious man I ever saw, and I could not help feeling almost afraid of him, and yet there was a fascination about him that made me like to see him. He was

very fond of quoting the classics, too fond also
of introducing Latin quotations in his prose
writing, and I had to tell him once that as a
rule sporting readers were more conversant with
Bell's Life or the *Druid* than with Horace or
Juvenal."

In August, 1869, he was appointed a steward
of the Melbourne Hunt Club, in company
with Major Barker, Messrs. G. Watson, H.
Power, J. Madden, and other well-known hunts-
men.

At last came the fateful news about the Esselmont Barony. He was terribly and painfully in
earnest in his hope of obtaining the estate and
its income of over £2,000 per year—not, indeed,
for himself, but for his wife. He had no antici-
pation of enjoying the wealth. " He felt," he
said on one occasion, " that his system was too
shattered to weather the storms of life long
enough for him to enjoy the ease and freedom
from pecuniary embarrassments that the income
would confer." His anxiety was for his wife. If
the entail held good the benefit would be hers.
She would be lifted far above the storm and
stress of poverty, and would reap a rich harvest
of peace and enjoyment after years of toil and
care and anxiety. This hope burst like a ray of
sunlight through the gathering gloom of his life.

It cheered his drooping spirits, and, freeing his mind from the anxieties of providing for the necessities of daily life, it gave a fresh impetus to the nobler instincts of a nature ever striving to find expression in verse.

> " A shining soul with syllables of fire,
>   Who sang the first great songs these lands can claim
>   To be their own."

Gordon consulted a local lawyer on the subject of his property, and received an encouraging opinion. Every effort was made to prove his right to the entail which had been bequeathed in 1864 by Charles Napier Gordon to his daughter, Mrs. Woolridge. After months of weary waiting, anxious hopes, and racking fears (but during which he prepared his most popular volume, " Bush Ballads and Galloping Rhymes "), Gordon received the heart-breaking news that the entail was rendered void by the " Entail Amendment Act " of 1848. This was a crushing blow. Just as he had been lifted to the highest pinnacle of hope, so was he dashed to the lowest depths of despair. " My poor wife, my poor wife ! " he exclaimed in his agony. The whole fabric of his bright vision vanished, and he had to face the stern realities of debt (incurred on the assumption of his being the legal heir) and the

lack of means to satisfy importunate creditors.
The world will never know the agony of that

> " Brave great soul
> That never told a lie, or turned aside
> To fly from danger."

On Thursday, the 23rd of June, 1870, " Bush
Ballads and Galloping Rhymes" was published,
and Gordon was shown by a brother poet—Kendall—a proof-sheet of a very favourable criticism
which was to appear in a leading newspaper.
This pleased him highly, and put him into a very
nervous state of excitement, which was accentuated
by the knowledge that on the following day he had
to meet a bill of £30, and had not the wherewithal
to satisfy the claim. Nothing unusual beyond
this excitement and general cheerfulness was noted
in his manner, but he unfortunately drank several
glasses of spirit during the afternoon, and became
very much unnerved. He was a man of extremely
temperate habits, and owing to the injuries he had
received was very easily affected by spirituous
liquor. Dr. J. O. Murray, who knew the poet inti-
mately, declared that he "was eccentric, but on
the whole rational, though subject to excitement
without adequate provocation, and was totally
unable to bear any spirituous liquor—a very small
quantity of which maddened him immediately."

It may also be noted here that no man led a more active, healthy, and temperate life, as he was a great walker and excellent swimmer, and could endure any amount of fatigue. At four o'clock in the afternoon, after having purchased some cart-ridges for the rifle which he possessed by virtue of his membership in the Brighton Artillery Corps, he parted from Kendall with the intention of going by train to his residence at Brighton, though he had previously made a practice of walking to save expense. He reached home about five o'clock, and took tea with Mrs. Gordon, who did not notice anything very peculiar in his manner. During the evening he conversed with Mr. Kelly about the corps, of which they were both members, and stated that he proposed having some shooting practice early next morning, as he had made a match with some person he did not name. He gradually became very restless and quarrelsome, and went in and out of the house several times before he retired for the night. Doubtless the brooding over his difficulties had whirled his brain into a chaos of frenzy and despair, for he saw no means of escape from the Scylla of poverty on the one hand, and the Charybdis of disgrace on the other.

The following morning, Friday, June 24th, he rose early, kissed his beloved wife, who, only seeming

conscious of his departure, soon fell asleep again.
He left the house about half-past seven, called at
the Marine Hotel, and asked for the landlord, his
friend, Mr. Prendergast, who, unfortunately, was
not up. Unfortunately, because Mr. Prendergast
would have noticed something strange in Gordon's
manner, and would in all probability have influenced him to return home. But it was not to be.

> " If the way had been shorter and greener
> And brighter he might have been brave,
> But the goal was too far, and he fainted,
> Like Peter with Christ on the wave ! "

He passed down Park Street, and the last man
to see the poet alive was a fisherman named
Harrison, who bade him " good-bye," to which
salutation poor Gordon, absorbed in his own
terrible thoughts, made no reply. He shortly after
turned into the thick scrub. He must then
have loaded his rifle, seated himself on the ground,
placed the butt of the rifle firmly in the sand
between his feet, put the muzzle to his mouth, and
with a forked ti-tree twig pushed the trigger.
The bullet passed through his brain, and

> " Out of his body for ever,
> Wearily sobbing, ' O whither ? '
> A soul that hath wasted its chances
> Floats on the limitless ether !

At nine o'clock the lifeless body was discovered and conveyed to the Marine Hotel.

Thus passed away one who has laid Australia under a deep and lasting obligation. Amongst the few writers of imaginative literature that Australia has produced, he certainly occupied no secondary position. "He has contributed what we believe," says the *Australasian*, "to be a durable addition to the treasures of the English language, and one that will be talked of long after this unquiet, unsettled generation has passed away."

> " Peace is best ! If life was hard,
>   Peace came next,
>   And the tried and tired bard
>   Lies unvexed.'

He was buried in the picturesque Brighton cemetery, and over his remains there has been erected a monument on " a gently sloping rise, fanned by the sea breeze, and looking towards the setting sun." It is in a wild and lonely spot, but frequently visited by pilgrim Australians, who stand and weep by the side of the grave of their " poor Gordon." The monument consists of a massive bluestone base, upon which rests a finely rubbed bluestone pedestal with handsomely moulded plinth. Upon each face of the pedestal die a polished white marble tablet is affixed, bearing the following inscriptions. On the front face :—

THE

POET

GORDON.

—

Died June 24, 1870.
Aged 37 Years.

On the other faces are the words :—

ASHTAROTH,
BUSH BALLADS
and
GALLOPING RHYMES,
and
SEA SPRAY
and
SMOKE DRIFT.

From a moulded base a fluted Doric column rises to the height of 10 feet above the ground. It is then broken off to illustrate the sad end of an uncompleted life. The whole is finished with a carved wreath of bay leaves in white marble. Jennings Carmichael, a rapidly rising Australian author, thus writes of " The Grave of an Australian Poet " :

" The scene about the grave of Adam Lindsay Gordon, who lies buried in the Brighton cemetery, is quite Australian in its calm and

uncultured beauty. The wild and solitary spot
is on an undulating slope overlooking a fair but
lonely landscape. The wind that rushes through
the depths of seeded grass blows over green fields
and hedges, and there are woods in the distance.
A shapely she-oak and a few young gums grow
near the tomb, but I saw no wattle, Gordon's
especial tree. There is not the ornamentation of
the St. Kilda cemetery, one of the most artistic of
burial-grounds, with its rocky ponds and wealth
of gorgeous flowers, but here we have instead the
best kind of beauty, where Nature is controlled
and yet untrammelled, and the pathetic mounds
rise in the midst of lavish verdure, strewn by fall-
ing petals from Nature's own garden, and shadowed
by Nature's own trees.

"The broken column, with its crowning wreath,
is an apt symbol for the life of our poet—so appropriate, indeed, that one feels a rush of tears to the
eyes and a wave of emotion to the heart when
seeing it.

"The warm wind blows across the clustered wild
flowers, and bends their sweet blossoms to the earth.
Overhead stretches an opaque sky, swept since
dawn by a fierce north wind that has opened wide
the discs of the dandelions, and cast a yellow tone
over the landscape. In the brown she-oaks birds
are twittering and glancing through the needled

branches. The whirr of passing trains and the monotonous beating of some distant drum comes on the senses as a reminder of that outside world which seems so far away in this quiet spot. For the world's pulse throbs but faintly in these grassy uplands set with gravestones and sown with flowers. Is it the voice of the sea we hear, or only the complaining stir of the wind in the trees? It were well if the ' wash of a wave ' were near enough to give the air the ocean savour so inseparably connected with the poems of Gordon. But the breeze, which every minute grows more vigorous, drowns the subtle echo that may sound when the elements are at rest. Unconsciously one's mood harmonizes with the surroundings, and it looks fitting that the grey column should stand out against an ashen sky, across which clouds are flitting. There is a sympathy in the wind as it moans through the boughs and sends a tremble along the ranks of tasseled grass, suggesting the passionate metres of one who so truly caught the strange music of the new world, and struck the keynote of Australian verse, which may reverberate undyingly through all the poetry of the future. For

> " ' Rhymes rudely strung with intent less
> Of sound than of words,'

are really the core of poetic thought, and it is only

From a Photograph by Mr. George Watson, of Mt. Gambier

OBELISK ERECTED AT MT. GAMBIER, S.A., NEAR
THE SITE OF "LINDSAY GORDON'S LEAP."

in looking beneath the surface of mere literary workmanship that the conscientious student of art finds the embryo spark of the divine fire—genius."

Eighteen years later another monument was erected to his memory at Mount Gambier. The obelisk is on the site of the famous leap to which reference has been made, about 20 feet above the Port MacDonnell Road, at an elevation that renders it visible from nearly every point of the Mount Gambier and Lake Reserves. The obelisk is about 20 feet high, the lowest base being of grey dolomite, rock-faced, and having a 15-inch plinth. It bears on the front the words, " Adam Lindsay Gordon." The foundation-stone was laid on July 8, 1887, Mr. John Riddoch, J.P., of Yallum, S.A., performing the ceremony. During an appropriate speech he referred to his " old friend Gordon " in the following terms :—

" Gordon was necessarily thrown a great deal into the society of sporting men, many of whom were his friends; but at the same time the conviction was forced upon him that many of that class were most undesirable companions, and he was led to fear that through their influence he might be led into doing some act that his conscience and high sense of honour would not fully approve. During the last years of Gordon's

life, when his popularity as a steeplechaser was at
its highest, when he as a rider was backed and
not the horse he rode, and when he was not in
affluent circumstances, many temptations were put
before him—temptations that to many similarly
placed would be irresistible.   But those who knew
Gordon best, however, would know he was far
above being tampered with, and that those who
might try to tamper with him would not go un-
scathed away.   What influenced him in his career
as a horseman was his great fondness for the
horse, the excitement of riding in a steeplechase,
and the honour and glory attendant upon the
victory.   Gordon's beautiful poems have become
known wherever the English language is spoken,
and his feats on the hunting field and as a steeplechase rider will be remembered in Australia for all
time.   This beautiful monument, of which we have
now laid the foundation-stone, in view of the scene
of one of the most sensational and wonderful feats
of horsemanship ever carried out in Australia, will
keep his memory green, at all events, in this town
and neighbourhood—a town and neighbourhood he
loved so much, and to which, as one of its representatives in Parliament, he gave an honourable
service."

"He is not unworthy," says one, " of his monument—not unworthy of a warm place in the hearts

of all those who have any love of bold manhood and spirit-stirring song. He is, indeed, an altogether remarkable figure in the first half-century of Victorian life." During the eighteen years that have elapsed since his death, his genius as a poet has received wider and wider recognition. It has spread from the little coterie of admiring turfites in a far-off corner of the island-continent of the Southern Seas to the great world beyond ; has overshadowed his reputation as a steeplechaser, and dwarfed into insignificance his fame as a hunter. His musical lyrics and his stirring ballads have been well described as seeming to flow from his mind at a white heat, and by the help of a fine ear for rhythm and a singular felicity of expression he was able to cast them into beautiful and appropriate moulds. The materials and the structure were alike excellent. Conspicuous among the merits of his verse was their robust vitality. He wrote like a man overflowing with vital energy, and revelling in that grateful sense of the blessedness of existence which is experienced by men of healthy frames and healthy minds.

I have no intention of entering into a detailed criticism of the poet's works; I have simply aimed to place before the public a memoir of his life that will gratify the desire for some fuller information than has hitherto been attainable. A few facts, however, concerning his work may be noted. Many of his verses appeared in *Bell's Life in Victoria*, the *Australasian*, and the *Colonial Monthly*. Towards the close of 1867 he published "Sea Spray and Smoke Drift," a copy of which was sent to Whyte-Melville, who acknowledged the receipt of the volume in the following terms :

"I have to thank you for a volume of poetry called 'Sea Spray and Smoke Drift.' Will you kindly convey to the author, when you see him, my sincere thanks for the pleasure he has given me. I know nothing more spirited, or with more dash about it in the language. The sentiments, too, are so manly and encouraging; while here and there one comes upon a couplet or stanza which will be quoted when most of us are forgotten. If your friend rides as well as he writes (and I am sure he is a real workman), I should like to put him up in any steeplechase for which I had a likely winner, and should be still more pleased to see him in the saddle with a good pack of fox-hounds. I think his ballads are equal to Warburton's Cheshire Hunting Songs, or even Charles Kingsley's Riding Stories. Can I say more ?"

The poet's next volume, "Ashtaroth," contains many beautiful lyrics, but it is doubtful whether it will ever become popular. It never will become a favourite in the sense that "The

Sick Stockrider," " How we Beat the Favourite,"
" The Lay of the Last Charger," are favourites.
On the 23rd of June, 1870, appeared his third
volume, " Bush Ballads and Galloping Rhymes,"
dedicated, in a beautiful poem, to Whyte-Melville.
Shortly after the issue of this book the *Austra-*
lasian (which certainly deserves the honour of
having " discovered " the poet) published a prose
tale under the title of " Bush Sketches." Gordon
once thought of trying his hand at novel-writing.
He was of opinion that an author in that line of
literature should take his rank according to the
impression he produced on a large number of
readers, and judged by that standard, says the
Rev. J. E. T. Woods, he placed Le Sage, Cer-
vantes, Sir Walter Scott, Manzoni, Dickens, and
Thackeray in the foremost place. He considered
Dickens to be deficient in thought, and without
any sensible view as to the principles of life and
conduct. He detested Fielding and Smollett, and
regretted that Thackeray had shown such contempt for menials, and considered this a "blot upon
the fine tone which ran through his writings."
Competent judges affirm that had Gordon written
sporting novels he would have made fortune as
well as fame.

Of the miscellaneous poems hitherto appearing
in the poet's collected works, the authenticity of

" A Voice from the Bush " has been doubted, and the late Marcus Clarke has been credited with inserting and altering a poem that was not written by Gordon. As a matter of fact, Clarke always had doubts as to Gordon being the author of the poem. Referring to the subject on one occasion, he said, " For my own part I do not think that Gordon wrote 'A Voice from the Bush' at all. The lines are spirited certainly, but rugged to a degree. Gordon's ear for rhythm was acute as is Kendall's or Swinburne's. The penultimate stanza, beginning ' I watch them, but from afar,' is surely not by the pen which wrote the ' Ballad of Britomarte.' " He further says : " Mr. J. C. F. Johnson and Mr. Lavington Glyde both write, however, positively asserting that Mr. Clark told them that the verses were written by Mr. Morris. ' When speaking to Mr. John Howard Clark about some verses of my own, " Found Dead," about the authorship of which a question was raised,' says Mr. Johnson, ' he distinctly told me that the poem now credited to Gordon was written by Mr. Morris.' Mr. Lavington Glyde is still more circumstantial. ' I well remember,' says he, ' saying to my old friend Mr. J. Howard Clark, " Who is your new poet ? " on the day when those verses first appeared as " Under the Trees " in " Geoffrey Crabthorne," for I recognized the

genuine ring of true poetry in them. He declined
to tell me, but on my pressing him, whispered " the
Cherub," as Mr. Morris was popularly called in
those days. I thought Mr. Clark joking at first,
but he *assured* me that Mr. Morris was the author,
and I believe his information was correct. Soon
after Mr. Morris left the colony I was surprised to
find the piece under the title of " A Voice from
the Bush," in *Temple Bar* of May, 1873.' Mr. J.
Walter Tyas stands up for the Gordon theory,
assuming that Gordon gave the verses to Morris,
and Morris gave them to Clark, who, naturally
enough, ascribed the authorship to the sender,
and backs his opinion by some cited passages,
which, if " A Voice from the Bush " was *not*
written by Gordon, certainly look much like
plagiarisms from his works."

Mr. Tyas writes: " In Gordon's stanzas entitled ' The Sick Stockrider ' occur the lines :

" ' With a running fire of stockwhips and a fiery run of hoofs,
Oh ! the hardest day was never then too hard !'

In ' A Voice from the Bush ' I find the following :

" ' Older, but men to whom
In the pride of their manhood strong ;
The hardest work is never too hard,
Nor the longest day too long.'

Again, in ' The Sick Stockrider' are the lines :

"'For good undone, and gifts misspent, and resolutions vain
   'Tis somewhat late to trouble. *This I know—*
  I should live the same life over if I had to live again,
   And the chances are I go where most men go.'

In ' A Voice from the Bush' the same sentiment
is expressed :

" ' Of the seed I've sown in pleasure,
    The harvest I'm reaping in pain ;
   Could I put my life a few years back,
    Would I live that life again ?
   Would I ? Of course I would ;
    What glorious days they were !'"

Again Marcus Clarke writes :

" Now it happens that I wrote a preface for the
first edition of ' Bush Ballads,' and this preface
being repeated in this present edition, I am not
unnaturally credited with the responsibility of
inserting the two poems in dispute. Indeed, Mr.
Johnson accuses me of purposely altering the
metre of ' A Voice from the Bush,' a freedom
which I certainly should not allow myself to take
with any author, unless for stated and defensible
reasons. The fact is that I never saw the verses
at all, until I read them in the issue of the
Advertiser for the 29th of September, which some
unknown friend in Adelaide was good enough to

send me. Inquiry at the publishers' has produced
but little satisfaction. They believe some ' friend '
sent the manuscript, but do not remember just
now his name."

These explanations ought to prevent any further
accusations of carelessness being hurled at the
memory of Australia's most famous novelist.

The poem is certainly Gordonesque in construction, and as claims to the authorship have been so
difficult to determine, the publishers have hitherto
permitted it to remain in Gordon's works.   There
is, however, indisputable evidence that the poem
was not written by Gordon, it having been em-
phatically claimed by Mr. Mowbray Morris, in a
a letter written some years ago to Major Ferguson
of the S.A. Rifle Brigade.   He writes :

" Certainly the verses are mine.   I remember
both the time and place where I wrote them,
lying on my back in a cave at Robe in the autumn
of 1871. . . . I was not aware that there
was any similarity, unconscious or otherwise,
to any verses of Gordon's.   I have two volumes
of his verse by me, and I cannot detect any conscious plagiarisms.   Certainly there were none
consciously committed.   Mine they are, every line
and every word, and they have no business among
the writings of any one else."

This settles the long dispute as to the authorship of that much-admired and much-debated poem, "A Voice from the Bush," or, as it was originally entitled, "Under the Trees." It will be parted from with some regret by admirers of Gordon, for, though defective in artistic finish, it bears a close similarity to the style of the master poet, and has been for many years accepted as a genuine example of his early "dalliance with the Muse." Marcus Clarke declared that "whoever wrote the lines the world is richer by them"—a high note of praise, surely, for Mr. Morris.

Thus may close a memoir, written by an Australian in loving admiration of a kind-hearted, honourable, but unfortunate gentleman and a true poet of rare merit and of surpassing promise.

NEW POEMS.

EXODUS PARTHENIDÆ.

THE LAY OF THE LAST SQUATTER.

DRAW your chair to the fire, old woman,
  The days are warm, but the nights are cold;
So, they've hunted our milkers off the common,
  And pounded them, calves and all, I'm told.
Had I caught " Long Henderson " driving
      " Molly,"
  I'd have made him tell me "the reason why";
He'd scarcely have answered you so jolly,
  Had I turned the corner suddenly.

Faith, 'tis time we laid our oars in the rullocks,
  We've got no right of commonage now, -
And the sheep are sold, and the working bullocks
  And the cattle, all but the strawberry cow;
I felt my heart for the moment soften
  When the butcher offered me three pound five
For the poor old thing that you've milked so
      often—
  She sha'n't be slaughtered while I'm alive.

And Robinson Brown has sent me his bill, dear,
   And Morton Jones has taken the lease,
And the kangaroo dogs, " Lion " and " Kildeer,"
   Are sold for fifty shillings apiece ;
I'm sorry to part with the red dog, truly,
   At fifty shillings I call him cheap,
But the brindled dog is a trifle unruly—
   Oh ! Carrington Jackson, mind your sheep.

I'm sure if Giles is satisfied, I am ;
   The horses averaged well, and though
I'd like to have kept the colt by " Priam,"
   'Tis just as well that I let him go ;
For if my creditors won't be losers,
   I've set them scratching their heads, mayhap,
And you know that some folk mustn't be choosers,
   Which folk I belong to—" *verbum sap.*"

I've had an interview with the banker,
   And I found him civil, and even kind ;
But the game's up here, we must weigh the
      anchor,
   We've the surf before, and the rocks behind ;
So trim the canvas, and clear the gangways,
   They've got the great unwashed on their side ;
It's no use sparring with " Templar Strangways,"
   It's no use kicking at " Lavender Glyde."

And I guess it's all U P with the squatter;
  The people are crying aloud for the land;
They've made it hot, and they'll find it hotter
  When they plough the limestone and sow the
    sand.
" All flesh is grass," so saith the preacher;
  " All grass is ours," quoth Randolph Stow;
Is the man related to Harriet Beecher?
  With *mobile vulgus* he's all the go.

And, years to come, in the book of Hansard,
  You may read the tale of the frogs retold,
How they prayed for a king, how their prayer
    was answered,
  How the king was crowned, and the frogs were
    sold,
How they ended, the schemes whose names were
    " Legion,"
  In the Mephistopheles laughter note,
From the depths of "the Mariner's" gastric
    region,
  That rattled up to his innocent throat.

I wish you'd write me a line to Maddox
  (My fingers are cramped with that boring brute);
I'll take his bid for the purchased paddocks,
  The sum we mentioned he won't dispute.

I might have made better terms with Parker
    If he hadn't known I was forced to sell,
But I couldn't have kept these matters darker,
    I didn't try to—'tis just as well.

Fred Carson made an offer for Lancer—
    'Twas a little less than his hide would bring ;
You may guess I gave him a civil answer,
    Which put a stop to his huckstering ;
I loosed the old nag at the sliding railing,
    And carried my saddle up to the hut ;
His eyes, as well as his limbs, are failing,
    He scarcely knew when the gate was shut.

Aye, troubles are coming upon us thickly,
    'Tis hard to leave the old place at last,
And you're not strong, and the baby's sickly,
    And your mother's ailing and aging fast.
I remember the days when credit was plenty,
    And years were few ; but those days are o'er ;
Old Beranger sings of the joys of twenty,
    But I shall never see thirty more.

It's no use talking, things might be better,
    And then again they might well be worse—
You needn't trouble about that letter,
    The youngster's squalling loud for a nurse ;

And your hand is surely rather unsteady,
    That writing looks to be all askew,
What ! are there tears in your eyes already ?
    Come, old girl, this will never do.

      *   *   *   *   *

I might have taken Time by the forelock,
    I might have made my hay in the sun,
I might have foreseen—but wizard or warlock
    Could never undo what once is done.
And at least I've wantonly injured no man,
    Although I've lived on the people's land—
Draw your chair to the fire, old woman,
    And mix a drop of the battle-axe brand.

THE OLD STATION.

AN UNFINISHED POEM.

ALL night I've heard the marsh-frog's croak,
   The jay's rude matins now prevail,
The smouldering fire of bastard oak
   Now blazes, freshened by the gale ;
And now to eastward, far away
Beyond the range, a tawny ray
Of orange reddens on the grey,
   And stars are waning pale.

We mustered once when skies were red,
   Nine leagues from here across the plain,
And when the sun broiled overhead
   Rode with wet heel and wanton rein.
The wild scrub cattle held their own,
I lost my mates, my horse fell blown ;
Night came, I slept here all alone :
   At sunrise, riding on again,
   I heard yon creek's refrain.

Can this be where the hovel stood
   Of old ?   I knew the spot right well :
One post is left of all the wood,
   Three stones lie where the chimney fell.
Rank growth of ferns has well-nigh shut
From sight the ruins of the hut.
There stands the tree where once I cut
   The M that interlaced the L—
   What more is left to tell ?

Aye, yonder in the blackwood shade,
   The wife was busy with her churn ;
The sturdy sunburnt children play'd
   In yonder patch of tangled fern.
The man was loitering to feed
His flocks on yonder grassy mead ;
And where the wavelet threads the weed
   I saw the eldest daughter turn,
   The stranger's quest to learn.

Shone, gold-besprinked by the sun,
   Her wanton wealth of back blown hair.
Soft silver ripples danced and spun
   All round her ankles bright and bare.
My speech she barely understood,
And her reply was brief and rude ;
Yet God, they say, made all things good
   That He at first made fair.

     *   *   *   *   *

[NOTE.—The manuscript here is rather blurred and in-
distinct, and probably the author's words are not accurately
copied, as the sense is rather vague.]

She bore a pitcher in her hand
   Along that shallow, slender streak
Of shingle-coated shelving sand
   That splits two channels of the creek ;
She plunged it where the current whirls,
Then poised it on her sunny curls,
Waste water decked with sudden pearls
   Her glancing arm and glowing cheek ;
   What more is left to speak ?

It matters not how I became
   The guest of those who lived here then ;
I now can scarce recall the name
   Of this old station ; long years, ten—
Or twelve it may be—have flown past,
And many things have changed since last
I left the spot, for years fly fast,
   And heedless boys grow haggard men
   Ere they the change can ken.

The spells of those old summer days
   With glory still the passes deck,
The sweet green hills still bloom and blaze
   With crimson gold and purple fleck.

For these I neither crave nor care,
And yet the flowers perchance are fair
As when I twined them in her hair,
   Or strung them chainwise round her neck.
   What now is left to reck ?

The pure clear streamlet undefiled
   Durgles (?) thro' flow'ry uplands yet ;
It lisps and prattles like a child,
   And laughs, and makes believe to fret,
O'erflowing rushes rank and high ;
And on its dimpled breast may lie
The lily and the dragon-fly.

* * * * *

[NOTE.—The manuscript, which is carelessly written and
unrevised, abruptly leaves off here.]

VÆ VICTIS!

BY "ONE OF THE LEGION OF THE LOST."

THERE was revel on Flemington Course,
   Clamour of tongues and clatter of feet,
Rider to rider and horse to horse,
   " 'Twas a China orange to Lombard Street."

There were bookmakers, trainers, touts,
   Heavy swells and their jockeys light,
The man that drinks and the man that shouts,
   Carrier pigeon and carrion kite.

Wheresoever the carcase lies,
   There will the eagles gather together,
And the shambles swarm with the summer flies
   That buzz and drone in the summer weather.

" Væ Victis! Woe to the conquered!
   Gone our luck is, lick'd we are ;
I warrant my friend ' Mr. Peter Prankerd '
   Would have made an investment safer far. "

For the partisans of Falcon quailed,
   And the backers of Barwon felt a chill,
And the stride of Lady Heron failed,
   And Cowra stopped, and Mozart stood still.

In the Stand the faces of many paled,
   And the pulses of many stayed on the hill,
When through his horses the Exile sailed,
   And raised the hopes he couldn't fulfil.

Tell it not in the city of gold,
   In Dowling Forest publish it not,
How he flagged and tired, the four-year-old,
   Long or ever a place he got.

He was black as the raven's wing,
   Black and yellow his rider's garb,
And I heard the " cabbage-tree " chorus sing
   A pæan loud to the conquering Barb.

" Væ Victis! Woe to the conquered!
   Shall we confess it, sooth to say,
'Twas after another colt we hankered,
   But he couldn't pull it off that day."

Who knows whether he might have won;
   He was beaten, every one knows. '
What does it matter? the race is run,
   P'r'aps he was taken bad with the slows.

Health and credit to Mister Tait,
   Honour and glory to New South Wales:
We hope against hope, we fight against fate,
   Those Sydney scrubbers will show us their tails.

And some must sow for others to reap,
   And some must frown for others to grin,
And some must watch that others may sleep,
   And some must lose that others may win.

Days of sorrow and days of mirth,
   Their pain and pleasure they mingle must;
What does it matter, boys?—earth to earth,
   Ashes to ashes, and dust to dust.

The vessel freighted with our hopes, split
   On a rock, and the reed we leaned on broke—
Ex nihilo nihil fit—
   And the dream of the Smoker ends in smoke.

"Nil desperandum!" Luck to the conquered,
   Better, it may be, another time.
Comrades all, here's luck in a tankard,
   Sift the reason out of this rhyme.

"I AM WEARY, LET ME GO."[1]

Lay me low, my work is done,
　　I am weary.　Lay me low,
Where the wild flowers woo the sun,
　　Where the balmy breezes blow,
Where the butterfly takes wing,
　　Where the aspens, drooping, grow,
Where the young birds chirp and sing—
　　I am weary, let me go.

I have striven hard and long
　　In the world's unequal fight,
Always to resist the wrong,
　　Always to maintain the right;
Always with a stubborn heart,
　　Taking, giving blow for blow;
Brother, I have played my part,
　　And am weary, let me go.

[1] "Australian Poets, 1788–1888." By kind permission of Messrs. Griffith and Farran.

Stern the world and bitter, cold,
  Irksome, painful to endure;
Everywhere a love of gold,
  Nowhere pity for the poor.
Everywhere mistrust, disguise,
  Pride, hypocrisy, and show;
Draw the curtain, close mine eyes;
  I am weary, let me go.

Other chance when I am gone
  May restore the battle call,
Bravely lead the good cause on,
  Fighting in the which I fall.
God may quicken some true soul
  Here to take my place below
In the heroes' muster-roll—
  I am weary, let me go.

Shield and buckler, hang them up,
  Drape the standards on the wall;
I have drained the mortal cup
  To the finish, dregs and all;
When our work is done, 'tis best,
  Brother, best that we should go —
I am weary, let me rest;
  I am weary, lay me low.

PROSE SKETCHES.

BUSH SKETCHES.

[A melancholy interest attaches to the following sketch, as it was handed in to the editor of the *Australasian* by the writer, Mr. A. L. Gordon, two days before he committed suicide. He stated that he had given the story very much as he received it under the circumstances described from the chief actors in it.]

WE were sitting, Thurstan, M'Pherson, and myself, in the overseer's hut that evening, when Norman came to the door to make some inquiries about the disposition of horseflesh for the morning, and was asked to come in and talk over some matters connected with the muster at " The Neck." The conversation, which was at first chiefly of a horsey character, diverged into another channel somewhat in this wise.

Norman.—If it wasn't for old Selim's back, he could carry your weight better and longer than anything you've got, M'Pherson.

M'Pherson.—There's a good deal of the Arab in his breed ; he's an Abdallah, you know, and his mother, you remember, was Brown's favourite hack, Zellika, or some such name.

Norman.—Zuleika, man; the name is taken from " The Bride of Abydos."

M'Pherson.—Ay, one of Moore's things, ain't it, or Burns's?

Norman.—No, Byron's; the man that wrote " Parisina," that Fletcher used to read.

M'Pherson.—I know. Yes, it wasn't bad stuff, some of it.

Thurstan.—" Parisina's " great rot; so are all the Oriental pieces of Byron's.

Norman.—Don't you like " Mazeppa," Ned?

Thurstan.—" Mazeppa's " a spirited tale in verse; not a poem, though there are a few snatches of poetry in it, perhaps; besides, " Mazeppa's " not an Oriental story.

Norman.—I hope you're not going to run down Byron.

Thurstan.—Not I. Byron will survive the English language, as Homer survived the Greek.

Norman.—Greek exists still.

Thurstan.—Well, you can't say that it lives; Greek is a dead language.

M'Pherson.—If you fellows are going to talk poetry and quote Greek, there'll be no more rational talk to-night.

Thurstan.—Well, we'll talk bullock if you like.

How did that strawberry stag with cock horns turn out I sold you? I've a mate of his for sale now.

M'Pherson.—Oh, bother bullocks; there was a question I wanted to ask you, but you've put it out of my head. What was it?

Thurstan.—I can't give you your dream and the interpretation thereof.

M'Pherson.—I had an argument with Lorimer; he was saying that the Sydney horses would do longer and faster work off grass than any others in the world.

Thurstan.—I never saw any real Arabs, but I should give these the preference from what I've heard. I've ridden a spotted mustang in the American prairies 180 miles in twenty-two hours, and he was not much the worse for it—in fact he was as well as ever in a week.

M'Pherson.—Tell us all about it, Ned.

Thurstan.—There's really nothing to tell. I was in a hurry. One of my mates was sick. Three of us were camped near the "Condor," at the furthest spur of the Rocky Mountains. We had no medicine, and our stores had run out. I rode to Swayne's settlement, got what I wanted, and returned on a fresh horse at the close of the fourth day. The Jaguar would have carried me back quicker.

Norman.—That's the horse you rode when the plains caught fire, isn't it?

Thurstan.—The same. I told you of that once. He was a long low horse, something the shape of your Doctor, but more massive, and much stronger. Talk about your stock horses; you should have seen him walk round a buffalo bull. I never crossed his equal. Poor Jaguar! I sha'n't easily forget the last time he carried me.

Norman.—Do give us that story, Ned, there's a good fellow?

M'Pherson.—Ay, it will liven us up a bit, and you too, Ned.

Thurstan laughed, a short dry laugh, and said, after a short pause:—

"You think it will enliven you up, do you? Well, there's no accounting for tastes. Now don't blame me. You've asked for it, and you shall have it. I've been dreaming about it these two nights running, and I've a notion that I shall dream of it again to-night if I keep it to myself; otherwise, I never have spoken of that occurrence, and I never intended to either.

"About twenty years ago I was the youngest of a party of five. We were returning from a sporting excursion, and we stopped at Henderson's hunting grounds, a station on a bend of the Little Fish River just above the big rapids. The two Hendersons were living on apparently friendly terms with a number of Indians, a branch of the

Seminole tribe. I had got hurt in a buffalo hunt, and while recovering I got a touch of a kind of prairie fever, which pulled me down a great deal, so I was glad of a rest, as indeed we all were. James Henderson, the younger brother, was an old comrade of mine; a terribly wild fellow he had been, but he was quieter then. Both he and his brother John were as hospitable as Bedouin chiefs, and I was well nursed, and soon rallied. My companions amused themselves for a fortnight and more, shooting and fishing, and sometimes mixing with the Indians, though Ramsay, the head of our party, was always rather suspicious of these. The chief was a very old man, and not a bad fellow for an Indian; at all events, he seemed really attached to the Hendersons, but he had an amiable weakness for fire-water, which plays the deuce with a white man, as we know, but cuts an Indian down like grass. He had a nephew called Little Bear, who was likely to be elected chief in event of the old man's death. This latter was no favourite with any of us, except John Henderson; there was something repulsive in his manner, though he was the smoothest-tongued rascal I ever met with. Ramsay said one evening to John, 'John, you ought to make tracks out of this! I wouldn't wait for the old chief to die if I were you. Take my word for it,

8

that Little Bear is a sneaking, treacherous skunk,
and unless I'm much mistaken, he's got some
grudge against you, for all he seems so fair.' The
elder Henderson replied carelessly, ' I suppose
James has put that idea in your head; he and
the Bear did have a scrimmage once, and it was
James's fault, but that's all forgotten, I fancy.
As for the old chief, he won't die for this many a
day—he's too tough.' Now both the Hendersons
had Indian wives, to whom they were, I believe,
espoused in Indian fashion; but John had also a
child by a former wife, an Englishwoman, who
had died in one of the Southern States. She, the
daughter, was quite a young girl, of perhaps ten
or eleven, and one of the prettiest and nicest
children I ever saw. She was a great favourite
of Ramsay's; in fact we all liked her. Ramsay
said, ' Look you, John, you ought not to let that
child grow up among the savages. I've got an
aunt at Boston who would be glad to take charge
of her.' Henderson replied, ' I can't spare Polly,
and she's clever enough. She does all my writing
for me now. What more do you want her to
learn? I don't intend to make a lady of her.'
Ramsay answered, ' Please yourself;' but he tried
again to persuade the other next day. Our party
were now preparing to make tracks across the
prairies to the stockade at Pipestone Quarry,

where Ogilvie, and Balfour, and a lot more friends
of ours were then living. Henderson persuaded
us to postpone our departure as long as he could,
but at last it was settled that we were to start
next day. I had been out that afternoon with
Conolly and Burton, and in a thick part of the
wood we had come suddenly upon Cora (as we
called her), John Henderson's Indian wife, and
Little Bear. They were talking earnestly, and
seemed quite startled when we surprised them,
but recovered themselves immediately. I should
have attached little import to this occurrence by
itself, if it had not been coupled with other
matters which aroused the suspicions of Ramsay,
and even of James Henderson. Little Bear had
a few days before borrowed from John all the
powder and lead that the latter could spare, with
a promise of speedy repayment, for a number of
the tribe who were going up the river on a shooting expedition. He had also set some of the
squaws to work digging a piece of trenchwork
opposite the white men's dwelling-house, supposed to be an aqueduct from the river to some
cultivated land of the Indians, for the purpose of
obtaining a supply of water for irrigation, and
such like, for Little Bear had mixed a good deal
with the whites, and pretended to understand
more about farming than most of us did. Still I

don't think any of us suspected any immediate
treachery. That night we were sitting round the
supper-table, when the elder Henderson said,
' Ramsay, I've been thinking over what you've
said about Polly, and she sha'n't grow up a wild
Indian. I can't spare her just now, and you won't
wait, but you'll stay some months at the Pipestone
Quarry. Tell you what I'll do. If you'll leave
Ned Thurstan here with us for a week, or ten
days at the outside, I'll ride with him to Balfour's,
and we'll take the child with us. Indeed, if I can
see my way to get out of this place, I don't know
whether I won't clear out of it altogether, and
take a trip to New York. What do you say? You
know Ned will be all the better for a little more
rest.' So after some talk it was settled that I was
to stay behind with the Hendersons for a week or
two, and then follow my companions. For my
own part I was contented either way. Next
morning I rode with Ramsay and the other three
for about eight or ten miles, and when we parted,
and I turned to come back, they gave me a bag of
bullets and nearly all their powder, knowing that
ammunition was so scarce at the hunting grounds.
When I got back I found that the old Indian
chief had died quite suddenly, and that both the
Hendersons had gone to the funeral ceremonies.
These I didn't care to attend, so I went fishing

with Polly. Nothing more of consequence occurred that day, but in the evening, the two
Indian women being absent, though the men had
returned, a dispute arose between the brothers,
and they had rather high words, James stating
openly that he had no faith in the Little Bear,
while John took that worthy's part, and accused
the other of prejudice and injustice towards the
Indian. Next day I was out on horseback in the
morning, and returning about noon I found James
alone in the house collecting all the firearms. He
said, ' Ned, don't let your horse go; put him in
the stable and give him a bite. I'll tell you why
presently.' I did as he suggested, and when I
rejoined him he remarked, ' I don't like the look
of things at all ; one of the women has taken our
canoe away, and we're almost defenceless. I
found out that there is to be a meeting of the
elders of the tribe to hold counsel to-day, and
John has not been invited. He never suspects
anything, and never will till it's too late. I believe that Little Bear has been stirring up the
Indians against us for some time. Of course he
could do little real harm while the old chief lived ;
now he can do almost as he likes. I struck him
once, and he never forgave me; more than this,
he hates us whites, but he's such a treacherous
varmint that you can't see through him at first.

We shall have to clear out of this, I'm thinking, and lucky if we do it with a whole skin. What ammunition have you got?' I produced my store, which proved much larger than he expected, and we loaded every rifle, carbine, and pistol on the place, and put them in the store-room, capped and ready for use. James added, ' If Polly were safe out of this I shouldn't care; we can take our chance if the worst comes. We'll keep your horse inside all night. I don't think they'll do anything till the rest of the tribe return, and they are not expected till to-morrow.' John Henderson came home rather late, and was rather surprised and even concerned when James told him that a council had been held without his knowledge. The younger brother added, ' Take warning, John, for once, and send the young one away to-night. If you won't go, let Thurstan take her on his horse. There'll be a scrimmage to-morrow as likely as not. That meeting to-day was something to do with us.' Henderson looked rather anxiously at the child, who was pouring out coffee at the time, and said, ' I would if I thought——' when who should walk in but Little Bear. The doors were always left open, and the Indians could come and go as they liked, and indeed their wigwams had been always open to us in the same way. The young Indian evidently wanted

to confer with the elder Henderson, and we left
the two alone, and went to smoke our pipes outside, it being a beautiful warm moonlight night.
In a little while the pair joined us, and after some
brief salutations the Bear took his departure.
Then John coolly informed us that the Indians
had held a meeting that day to discuss some
means for propitiating their white brother, having
heard some rumour of his departure from among
them, and that it had even been proposed to elect
him chief in conjunction with Little Bear, who
expressed himself most anxious to share the
honours with him. He continued, ' You'll find
you've been wrong, James. The young chief will
be a truer ally to us than the old one was.' James
laughed incredulously, and his brother got angry.
The child was standing near us at the time, and
he said, ' If you're really afraid, you'd better go,
James.' ' Let the child go, John,' replied his
brother. ' Indeed,' answered John, ' Polly's not
frightened, if you are. Tell him so, Polly.' The
young girl laughed. She was a tall, strong, active
child, always in rude health, and naturally fearless. She had been used to Indians from her
infancy almost, and they had seemed fond of her.
She said, ' Uncle James, you're not really afraid
of Indians, are you ? ' When James and I were
alone he told me that he was sure the new chief

only came to play the spy, and to throw us off our guard. 'You'll see,' he added, 'we shall be attacked to-night. They think we have no ammunition, and they won't even wait till the hunting party returns. I shall keep watch.' So we agreed to watch alternately, but the night passed off quietly enough. The house was a long, low, log building of one storey, built in a bend of the river and close to the water, surrounded by a strong double - timbered palisade fence, quite 10 feet high, and loopholed. There was a door in the front, which when barricaded was as strong as any part of the fence, and another which opened on to the river at the back. The place could only be attacked by boats in the rear, as the palisade jutted into the water on each side. The stable was a mere shed built against the back of the house. Towards morning I began to think that the elder brother was right after all, and I was just lying down to get a short sleep when James roused me up. 'Quick,' he said, 'and help me to get out the guns. We're in for it now.' We soon carried out the firearms, and standing on a platform of plank which was built inside the palisade, I saw about seventy Indians in war paint, and armed with guns, hatchets, and knives. John Henderson came running out, half-dressed, and when he saw the aspect of affairs he took it much cooler than I should have expected. 'You're right, James,' was all he said. An Indian woman came forward and made signs of parleying, and she and John conferred through a loophole, but I did not hear what passed. Presently she went back. 'Did they offer any terms?' inquired James. 'Terms be ——,' replied his brother; 'we must fight now as long as we can.' When the Indian woman got back to the men, they set up a war whoop and came on at a run. Then we began to pick them off, and our firing rather astonished them, as they had expected to find us almost without ammunition. The child Polly came out at the report. She did not seem very frightened, or she didn't show it. Her father called her and made her load for him. We had twelve or fourteen rifles, some double-barrelled. She could load as fast as any of us, but I never saw her fire. The Hendersons were strong, determined men, and terrible shots. I don't think either of them wasted a bullet. We had no escape. I don't know whether we could have crossed the river above the rapids in a canoe if we had had one, which we hadn't. The Indians came within thirty yards of the palisade; then they broke and retreated to the dry trench, where they were under cover. Then we had a little breathing time, and we got all our pieces loaded again. Henderson, whose ears were keener than those of any savage, heard the sweep of a paddle in the rear. We ran round and found five savages trying to land and climb the palisade from a canoe in which they had crept under the bank. I jumped on the platform and emptied two revolvers, twelve shots, among the five, and killed two dead and crippled the rest. One stood up and tried to paddle clear, but he got into the swirl of the rapids, and was carried away and drowned. If the enemy had made an attack at that moment with their whole force they must have carried the place, but they couldn't see what was going on at the back from where they were. The Little Bear took good care of his own hide, for he was never forward in the first attack, and in the second he never showed at all. A young brave whom we called Tom, and who was said to have white blood in him, led on about twenty of the savages in a very determined manner. We shot several of them, but they came on to the fence, and tried to climb over it. Johnson, a reckless, daring young fellow, ran round the enclosure to the river side. Stooping below the loopholes, he made a spring, and catching the top of the palisade, swung himself up till he could throw one leg over. Another Indian handed him a gun, and he fired at James Henderson, who was nearest to him. James

turned and shot him dead, upon which his companions ran back to the trench, leaving several
dead and dying on the ground. John shot down
two in the retreat, emptying his last charges.
Our ammunition had been placed ready for instant
use in two open wooden boxes. I was stooping
to load one of the pieces, when I found the box
nearest me had been emptied, and going to search
the other, I was startled by a cry from Polly. I
turned my head, and saw the younger Henderson
leaning against the fence, holding his side, with a
face that grew whiter every instant. I ran to
him, but he fell before I reached him. His
brother was at his side the next moment. He
had been struck below the left armpit, by the
half-blood's bullet, probably, and mortally hurt,
both lungs being perforated. When we raised
him he made signs for water. Polly ran into the
house and brought some, and after a long draught
James beckoned to his brother, who knelt beside
him. I heard the words, which were jerked out
painfully through bubbles of bloody froth : 'Our—
ammunition—is—done. John, don't let Polly be
taken alive.' John nodded, and grasped his hand.
Then he said something to the child, who again
entered the building, the roof of which was now
catching fire, some arrows with flaming flax
wrapt round them having been shot from the

trench.   We placed the dying man against the
fence, and searched the ammunition boxes; there
was a little powder in one, but not a single bullet.
Henderson found a revolver with one chamber
loaded.   Polly had rejoined us with a flask of
spirits—rum, if I remember rightly.   John held
it to his brother's lips, but the latter shook his
head feebly; then he offered it to me, and I
refused; then he put the flask to his mouth and
nearly emptied it.   He said, 'Come here, Polly;
this has to be done, and it's no use putting it off.'
The child knew what he meant when he cocked
the revolver opposite the loaded chamber.   She
only said, 'Oh, father!' once, and gave him both
her hands, looking straight into his face with her
large eyes wide open.   He said, 'Shut your eyes,
girl!' and put the muzzle to her forehead.   I
struck up the barrel, and it exploded harmlessly.
'Stop, you fool!' I cried; 'she may be saved now.
Take my horse, and put her up behind you; you
can escape by the river.   You can't swim across,
but you can drift under the bank to the first
landing-place; then take to the woods.   They'll
see you, and fire, but the chances are they'll miss.'
He replied, 'Get your horse, quick; I never
thought of that.'   I soon brought the Jaguar out
saddled and bridled.   By this time the savages
had been reinforced by about forty of the hunting

party, who it seems had returned. 'Now,' said John, 'you're lighter than me, and a better rider; you must take the child. Before I trust her to you, you must swear that she sha'n't be taken alive if you can help it.' He was loading a small single-barrelled pistol with the remaining powder. I swore as he required. We had no lead, and there were no pebbles in the yard. Henderson gave me a bullet mould, saying, 'Draw one of my teeth.' I tried, awkwardly enough, and failed. Polly said, 'Take one of mine, father,' and (here Thurstan coughed huskily) he did it, and finished loading. Then I mounted my horse, and he fastened the child behind me, waist to waist, with his belt and a stirrup leather. He said, 'Remember your promise, and don't you be taken alive either, if you take my advice;' and he gave me the pistol and opened the river gate. The Jaguar slid quietly into the dark swelling water, and I saw no more of the Hendersons. Their scalps were hanging at Little Bear's girdle half an hour afterwards, but neither of them were taken alive, I'm sure. The river was clear, but an alligator could hardly have swam across so close to the rapids, and it was half a mile wide. My horse struck out well, heading down the stream close to the bank. There was a shelf of sand not sixty yards down, where canoes were sometimes kept.

Here we landed without difficulty, just as the Indians on our left were advancing to the building, the roof of which was now all in flames. They ran, and shouted, and fired. We were broadside on to them for a little way rounding a patch of reeds, then we turned our backs to them. The Jaguar gave a snort and a plunge, but never slackened speed, and the child clung closer, with a slight sob. I didn't think either of them were hurt to speak of. In a few strides we were out of their reach, and I never drew bridle for thirty miles, when we reached a small stream not far from the edge of the prairie. There we halted, and I found that the girl had been shot through the foot and couldn't stand. I bandaged the broken bones as carefully as I could, and while I was doing this the Jaguar went into the stream, and plunging his head up to the eyes in the water, drank till I thought he'd burst himself. When he came out he just fell dead; a bullet had entered his flank, and he had been bleeding internally all through that desperate gallop. I carried the child about five miles up the stream, which diverged into three or four channels, and to baffle the tracks walked knee-deep most of the way. I knew the Indians would get their horses and follow, though but for that unlucky shot they would never have come near us. Perhaps they saw tracks of blood as they rode; certainly when they found the dead horse they would redouble their search. I left the stream at last and found a good hiding-place, and in the night I struck the prairie and walked about thirty miles, carrying the child all the way. She couldn't put her foot to the ground, of course. So I travelled on, walking day and night with my burden in the direction of the Pipestone Quarry; but it was a long journey, and we had no water after we left the stream on the verge of the forest. On the third evening we reached a sandhill called the Bison's Back, where a well was, but it was quite dry. The summer had been unusually hot, and we had had a long drought—a rare thing in those parts. I was in hopes of finding a little water next day at a small lagoon; but I was disappointed again. The child had never complained, and even then seemed in good spirits, but she sobbed in her sleep a good deal that night. What's the use of talking about it! I made the Pipestone Hills on the fifth morning somehow or other, or I shouldn't be here to tell the tale." (Thurstan stopped suddenly, and M'Pherson asked some question, but he went on as if he hadn't heard it.) "I reached the first hillock a little after daylight. I had only two miles to go then, but I felt her getting chilly in my arms. At a clump of tall trees in sight of the station I tried to rouse her up. I said, 'Wake up, Polly; we're all right now!' and shook her. No use." (Thurstan paused again, and his face twitched nervously.) "There, you know it all now" (he continued). "I remember our fellows crowding around me, and, ah God, you should have seen their faces when they found out what I was carrying. I say, Mac, old fellow, I shall have the horrors if I dream of that again."

M'Pherson took a bottle of whisky from a box, and put it on the table. "Thank you for your story, Ned," he said, "and help yourself; that's good, you'll find."

Thurstan certainly did help himself rather bountifully, and adding water more sparingly, drank his dose with evident relish.

"Ah, well," he added, "we had a great revenge; it was worth living for. When Polly was laid out, Ramsay cut off some of her hair, and divided it with Marsh, Burton, and Conolly, and they all swore to have an Indian scalp for every separate hair that they held. I don't know that they all kept their oaths, but they went as near it as they could. We mustered pretty strong at the Quarry Station, and some of our boys were awkward customers when their blood was up. Ah, by heaven, but we had a great revenge. There was a queer old fellow among us, a New Englander,

Long Potter, or Parson Potter we called him, half Quaker, half Methodist. He was a terrible fellow among the buffaloes, and had tackled a grizzly single-handed, but he was always preaching forbearance and forgiveness of injuries towards the poor Indians. However, he had lived for a while with the Hendersons, and was very fond of poor Polly. At the child's funeral Ramsay turned to him and said, ' Now, old man, will you say " Vengeance is mine, saith the Lord " ? ' and Potter replied ; ' No, by God I won't ; if you are to be instruments of wrath, work your will in God's name.' Then he turned away and burst out crying, and some more of the men were nearly as bad. Now I'll turn in, for mark you, we must be up at the first grey streak to-morrow. I shall sleep sound, I think, so let the first man call me."

We were all soon in bed. I gave up my berth to Thurstan, and slept in the store on a shake-down ; but I slept ill, and was up long before daylight. Strolling outside I saw Norman smoking his pipe, and we chatted to pass the time. Norman remarked, " That story was not exaggerated in the least. I never heard it before ; but whatever faults Thurstan has he never draws the long-bow. I believe every word of it." (If I have made this tale sound strained or sensational, the fault lies with me, for as I and others heard it that night, there was an air of simple truth and even of feeling about it that carried conviction.)

I went to call the others in the overseer's hut at the earliest dawn, and found M'Pherson already up; but Thurstan was sleeping like a child, and was not easily awakened. Thinking afterwards over these things, and the events that were doomed to take place in a few hours, I can only express a hope similar to that expressed by one of the greatest of modern poets—

> " That after last returns the first,
> That what began best can't end worst,
> Nor what God once blest prove accurst."

RACING ETHICS.

THE historian Gibbon managed to fill six or eight large volumes with the details of the decline and downfall of the Roman Empire, and to the majority of readers it would probably be a laborious task to peruse the entire work from end to end. Not that Gibbon is a dull or prosy writer—rather the contrary; but the subject on which he expatiates at such length is somewhat wearisome. Gradual decay, slow but sure, is scarcely a pleasant picture to contemplate in any aspect.

It has been the fashion from time immemorial to extol the past and to decry the present. We are so used to this that we are apt to treat somewhat lightly the refrain of "the good old times," "the brave days of yore," &c., which our seniors occasionally inflict upon us. Argive and Larysæan, Salaminian and Boeotian, alike listened patiently, if not attentively, to the heroics of old Nestor; yet, perchance, when the ring of those grand hexameters had died out of their ears, they secretly voted the Pylian sage a bit of a bore, and indulged in grave doubts as to whether the leaders of his youth were any better than their own champions.

The decline of the turf is still an open question, and in any case the downfall of the same can hardly come to pass in our time, and is therefore a question that concerns us little. To all people, civilized, semi-civilized, or barbarous, sport of some description is a necessity. *Panem et circences* were the two things esteemed indispensable by the Romans of old. True enough, the amphitheatre has disappeared. Net and trident are no longer pitted against blade and buckler; Clodius and Apicius have ceased to pile the sestercia on their favourite gladiators ; and no traces are left of the oval sward strewed thickly with the yellow sands—

> " Ring'd round with a flame of fair faces,
>   And splendid with swords."

But these changes only came to pass when internal dissensions and barbaric inroads had sapped and undermined the dynasty of the Cæsars, when long ages of effeminacy and profligacy had left scarce a vestige of the ancient leaven to the degenerate descendants of the old Quirites, the progeny of the she-wolf's foster-child.

Prophets, not without honour even in their own

country, have lately girded up their loins and arisen against us. The Dean of Carlisle is no longer alone in the fray. The voice of one crying in the wilderness is swelled by the hum of many voices. Even that muscular Christian to whom, as the author of " Tom Brown's Schooldays," we would fain forgive much, has taken up his parable against the turf and all appertaining thereto. " Can a man touch pitch and remain undefiled ? " he asks. Well, pitch is bad enough, but there are nastier things than pitch to our way of thinking. The worst of all this is that we know that a great deal of what these men affirm is more than half true, and yet we, who pride ourselves on being like Hamlet, " indifferent honest," sit still or fold our hands and turn our backs, knowing that we have amongst us trainers that rope and grooms that poison, horse-jockeys that sell their own masters, and horse-masters that sell the public and suborn their neighbours' jockeys. Now and then, when an Oddstocking or a Blair Athol comes past the stand, pulling double, open - mouthed, over a winner, severely punished and sorely distressed, we feel compelled to express our disapprobation of such a barefaced bungle, and really the man who can't pull a horse without making a glaring exhibition of himself deserves all he gets, and a little more. But these cases are exceptional. As a rule, everybody except the immediate victim is satisfied with the benefit of the doubt and the verdict of "not proven."

Is it worth our while to analyze the good and evil in a thing that we must accept as a necessity, seeing that all the good is only comparative, and that perhaps all the evil is necessary, though it only be as a foil to set off the good? It seems that we argue this way, seeing that after the fashion of Gallio (whose conduct, by the by, is not highly commended) we "care for none of these things." The hell-keeping bookmaker or book-making hell-keeper, who combines cunning with cowardice and ruffianism with roguery, may surely outrage our self-respect (if we have any) till something more than a mild vote of censure escapes us. Some of us, at least, may say with Guy Livingstone's friend the Colonel, "We don't preach against immorality; it is brutality that seems to us simply disgusting."

Omnibus in malis, &c., a stale quotation, but nevertheless a true one. Even "three-up" may point a moral, though it can hardly adorn a tale. Perhaps, on the whole, we are not much worse than our forefathers; and, notwithstanding a few dissenting voices, I hold to what I believe to be the general opinion, that the turf has fostered and matured our breed of horses, and made them what

they are. Men will not go to the expense and labour
of breeding and rearing first-class blood stock, nor
will purchasers be found for the same, unless re-
munerative prizes are to be competed for. To
what, if not to the turf, is the superiority of the
English horse to be mainly attributed? To a
comparatively weak infusion of Arab blood introduced long ago, and crossed with the heavy
descendants of the great Norman destriers, or
the still more unwieldy Flanders-bred animal?
Scarcely. When the Moors overran Spain, they
distributed throughout the south of that country
a considerable number of Barbs and half-bred
Arabs, and the Spanish horse to this day shows
some traces of the Arab strain; yet what man
standing in need of a well-bred weight-carrying
hunter, or a powerful, high-couraged charger, or
even a first-class carriage horse, would go to
Spain? Probably neither the Godolphin nor the
Darley were pure Arabians, neither was the Byerly
Turk; and though our thoroughbred stock are derived from these, their qualities are rather owing to
the care and attention lavished upon them than to
hereditary excellence. Our national sports have
made our horses fit for war and for the chase, as
well as for the turf; while the national sport of
Spain, the horse-butchering bull-fight, has made
the Spanish horse fit for that and little else.

I believe to a great extent in Arab blood, if the same could be got pure, but I doubt whether a pure Arab has ever yet set foot on English or Australian soil. By the pure Arab I mean neither the Turcoman nor the Barb, the Persian nor the Syrian, still less the half-caste Arabs of India, but the true breed of the desert, the Arabian proper, such as we may imagine at this moment to be feeding near the tent-pegs of some Bedouin Scheik, such as we fancy Hakim and the Knight of the Leopard to have ridden in their flight from the soldiers of the Temple, such as may have borne the wild followers of the prophet of Mecca when, led by the impetuous Ali, they broke through clouds of battle-dust. There is something mythical and legendary in these horses; we have heard of them enough, and read of them, but which of us has seen them? And yet, according to Palgrave and others, these are the horses that fill the Nedjid stables. But from all accounts they are not easy to get to, and next to impossible to get hold of, so it seems we must do without them.

A great deal has been lately written concerning the deterioration of our horses, and doubtless many of them are worthless weeds: the increase of stock, and the difficulty of finding a market for the same, is detrimental to everything below the average. Speaking as far as my own colonial experiences extend, some fourteen or fifteen years ago I recollect a certain class of horse that was then common and is now rarely seen, if not almost extinct. For a long hurried journey or for a severe cattle muster, a man could desire no better mount than the well-bred Sydney stock-horse, and a first-rate animal was frequently picked at hazard even out of the mobs that came overland into Victoria and South Australia. A plain, resolute-looking head, lean neck, and rather lengthy forehand, with good girth and barrel, square, sinewy quarters, and clean flat legs, were the characteristic points of these horses. I remember one, a dark brown with a tan muzzle, that was once in the stables of the police troopers, and that upon one occasion carried a man of more than medium weight a distance of 200 miles in a little over forty hours, and was none the worse for his work; also another of the same stamp, a blue roan, that went all through the gold escort, and barring the almost inevitable sore back, showed no blemish whatever. I think this horse might have been matched to walk, trot, gallop, jump, and swim against anything in the colonies, best three out of five; and many others. I fancy these animals must have been the results of some fortunate nick of the acclimatized English blood with the half Arab, and I doubt whether they can be excelled

for endurance, combined with activity, by any that
we now possess. Still we have some horses faster
and stronger and more valuable than these were,
and we have others quite as useful for most
purposes. Violent journeys in the saddle are not
as indispensable as they used to be, and a cattle
muster nowadays is a comparatively tame affair,
and the worst weeds of the present time are no
worse than the three-cornered vicious brutes, fit
only to carry a pack-saddle or a roughrider, that
were once so prevalent. In those days some of
the best hacks and stock-horses were a little
uncertain of temper, and after a long spell at grass
an indifferent horseman would often fortify his
saddle with an article termed a " kid," that was
more useful than ornamental; and even a good
rider would not always disdain to strap his coat on
in front of him, when a strong crupper and a sur-
cingle, as well as an extra girth, were thought
requisite to keep the pigskin in its place.

Many of our racehorses especially are fit for
nothing but the off chance of pulling off some
light handicap in which they may be turned loose;
still, the winner of a three-mile race at weight for
age is usually of such a stamp that horses capable
of carrying a fair weight to hounds may yet claim
him or her as sire or dam; and it sometimes
happens that a light, undersized thoroughbred

whose performances on the flat have been considerably below par, becomes, through a fortunate nick, the parent of more than one first-class hunter. King Alfred, the sire of more really useful horses than almost any stallion in Victoria, is himself an ordinary-looking little horse. There is nothing very taking in his appearance beyond a certain evenness of shape, and the chances are that (had he been tried) he would have proved a failure on the turf, yet I know men who would send a favourite mare to him in preference to Fisherman, were the famous son of Heron still to the fore.

But, better or worse than they have been, our horses are good enough for the men that use them. It is not their possible decline or improvement that I wish to dwell upon principally at present. As long as there are good prizes to be contended for, there will be plenty of good horses to compete for the same. In spite of all the charges that are brought against the turf, most of which are not easily refuted, while many are unanswerable, it is the turf to which we feel ourselves indebted for such superiority as our horses still possess.

Taking this view of the case, we excuse ourselves for our apathetic endurance of offences which seem unavoidable though they may be committed openly, *sub die et coram publico.* Shall

we give vent to our anger merely because some
notorious knight of the pencil, whose foul mouth
speaketh out of the fulness of his fouler heart,
makes use of language unfit for any ears, especially
in a grand stand where respectable persons of
both sexes have assembled to keep holiday? This
man has a right to the enclosure as well as ourselves, and it is only natural that when suddenly
elated or rudely depressed he should give vent to
his feelings in the dialect which he and his boon
companions so much admire. Tastes differ, you
know—

"Pastilles Rufillus olet, Gorgonius hircum."

Rather a coarse quotation that, but fitted for the
topic; for the benefit of certain turfites I've a
good mind to translate it.

And yet before we dismiss this part of our
subject we may do well to inquire whether we
have not within our reach some possible remedies
for many of the evils which a system of wholesale
gambling and a consequent introduction of a tribe
of unscrupulous sharpers have engrafted on the
turf. Let us take breathing time and look around
us.

Once upon a time, before the steamhorse had
obtained footing on English soil, a certain stage
coach held four inside passengers. One of these,

a stout lady, turning to a gentleman seated next her, begged him to open the window; he complied, of course, but a thin lady sitting opposite complained of the draught, and insisted on the window being shut; the gentleman obeyed with alacrity, but the change had scarcely been effected when the corpulent fair one cried out that she was dying of suffocation, and should instantly expire unless the window was re-opened; and re-opened it was accordingly. The next moment the more attenuated female protested that the cold air was killing her, and that she was just on the point of death. The gentleman being puzzled, not to say perplexed, applied to the fourth occupant of the carriage, a friend who had hitherto taken no notice of the discussion. "What shall I do?" he inquired; "if I shut the window to save one lady's life I shall kill the other." His travelling companion made answer, "Keep it open till one dies, and then keep it shut till the other dies, and we shall have peace."

The moral of this anecdote is rather far-fetched, but shortly after the last New Year's meeting I heard an acquaintance remark, "One-half of our bookmakers are defunct, and it would be a good job if the other half would follow;" we've choked the first lot by taking the odds freely; now if we can only go in for a total abstinence from betting

for a few months, possibly we may starve the
residue, a consummation most devoutly, &c.   I
fear we lack self-denial sufficient for the carrying
out of our friend's suggestion, and those that have
been proof against asphyxia will scarcely perish
through inanition ; and besides this, the majority
would be against us.   We must admit the stale
truism of your correspondent, " The Old Commissioner," that racing and betting are inseparable,
having on a former occasion said as much ourselves.   We will not argue the point with the same
authority, when he informs us that bookmaking
may be as honourable an occupation as any
other, &c.   Perhaps bookmaking, when conducted
on an established principle, is not gambling in
the strict sense of the word, though based upon the
gambling propensities of others.   A good bookmaker may be a better man than a bad clergyman,
and we have good bookmakers amongst us.   If
all the layers of odds were of the same stamp as
the host of the Hunt Club Hotel and a few others,
we should have scant cause for complaint as far
as they are concerned.

But there are men who wager openly, and do
their business without let or hindrance, and whose
disreputable practices bring discredit upon all
whose profession may be in any respect identical
or even similar.   These are the carrion birds of

the turf, who hover to and fro on the confines of
the ring, seeking for the corpses upon which they
may gorge themselves to repletion. Nor is the
power which they sometimes wield contemptible,
whatever their persons may be. Their ill-gotten
gains, secured by their unhallowed calculations,
and strengthened by their unholy alliances, give
them an amount of evil influence, which, if fairly
gauged, would astound the uninitiated. Like the
Choosers of the Slain in Norse traditions, they are
not unfrequently able to select for themselves, in
which case they doom the quarry that appears
fattest in their eyes. Almost every tyro in racing
lore knows that a horse not meant for a race is,
as far as his chance of winning that event goes,
virtually dead, for though winning is always more
or less doubtful, there are fifty ways in which a
horse can be made safe, *i.e.*, certain to lose, from
scratching at the post to carrying false weight;
therefore sentence of death is hardly ever carried
out literally, as the "dead un" (to use the eloquent
phraseology of the Welshers) that comes to life
may be useful to fill the same post, and enact the
same part again. And yet the mysterious fate of
Exile would favour the supposition that there are
men on the turf that will stop at absolutely
nothing. True, we have no positive proof that the
horse was poisoned, or even tampered with, but a

more suspicious case has seldom occurred. I do not think myself that arsenic was the cause of death, because I have always understood that this mineral kills painfully, and by no means suddenly, by destroying the membrane of the stomach; but be this as it may, there is little doubt that foul play of some sort was resorted to.

It is one thing to point out grievances and another thing to devise remedies for the same. I fear I must shirk the second part of my question, though self proposed. I am not equal to the task of reform, and I have no feasible plan of redress to offer; therefore, if I've unwittingly raised any vague expectations to the contrary, I cry *mea culpa*, and retract. One or two wild projects have been suggested to me, as, for instance, the possible organization of a committee of gentlemen for the protection of the racing community, and the discovery, punishment, and suppression of malpractices—in short, a kind of "Amateur Turf Detective Force." Fancy Charlton Lennox, Esq., disguised as a seedy tout, fraternizing over gin and bitters with Simeon FitzSwindle, and trying to pump that worthy. Imagine the watery twinkle of amused penetration in FitzSwindle's bloodshot optic, and the suppressed chuckle with which he would put the swell on the wrong scent, and probably bring him to grief, though Charlton

can take his own part with the ordinary run of
men. I'm afraid it wouldn't work; the fact is,
Simeon and his colleagues are too clever for us.
Let us give them as wide a berth as possible,
and leave them to their own devices. They are
tolerated, I suppose, because they are solvent, and
solvency covereth a multitude of sins; but in spite
of their caution, their notoriety steadily increasing,
renders them less dangerous than they have been.
Of course it is a great pity to see young Pye John
Green arm in arm with Judas Fleecer, knowing
what he must assuredly know of Fleecer's ante-
cedents and occupations, but Pye John will live to
be a sadder and wiser, if not a better man, and as
for those by whom offences come, though they
escape detection for a while, they must reap their
own reward sooner or later. Let us quit this part
of our theme. Perhaps, when all is said, the turf
is not so black as we would paint it, and even if
otherwise, while many are content to accept it as
it is, and the rest are either callous or incredulous,
we can do little good by a jeremiad—

" Frustra fatigamus remediis ægros."

To turn to a pleasanter subject. The new pro-
grammes of the V.R.C. seem to give general
satisfaction, and the abolishment of the great
gathering on New Year's Day is surely a step

in the right direction. It was rather too much of a good thing under the blazing midsummer sun, and over the parch'd earth baked to the consistency of a brickbat. The Champion Race was a severe trial upon the best horses of the day, and the Grand National was almost cruelty to animals ; the sport was always good, but what is sport to some may be death to others, and a "merciful man is merciful to his beast." We have not much to cavil at now. The old vexed question of handicaps versus weight-for-age races has been used up and set aside. Doubtless, weight for age is the fairest criterion of merit, but handicaps are deservedly more popular, to say nothing of the increased competition. Many a really good animal would be untried and unknown were the inducements of a light burden withheld. We have now a tolerably fair proportion of both kinds, and though it cannot be denied that young stock are frequently injured materially by severe races at two and three years old, yet horse-breeders would lose half their stimulant were these stakes done away with.

There is one branch of our national sports which ought to be the connecting link between the racecourse and the hunting-field, and here, at least, some alterations may surely be effected. In England, steeplechase handicaps are often much

too light, but there the courses are light also, and
the weeds are able to carry their feathers at racing
pace through the thin straggling hedges and low
rotten fences with a comparatively small percent-
age of serious accidents. In England, too, steeplechasing is confined to the winter or the early
spring, and the soft ground is favourable to the
legs of the horses and the bones of their riders;
here we have the evils of the home system without
the advantages. Our handicaps are adjusted on
such a scale that many of our steeplechasers have
to carry light stable boys, who are not strong
enough to steady them, over ground nearly as
hard as a macadamized road, and a succession of
fences every one of which seems to have been
constructed for the express purpose of throwing
the horse that fails to clear it. Steeplechasing is
of course intended to be a dangerous pastime, but
the sport is scarcely enhanced by making it as
dangerous as it can be made. "Faugh-a-Ballagh"
or "Market Harborough," or some other fire-
eating bruiser may read this, and observe that the
writer is evidently one of the soft division, and
they may be right, but I confess I do not care to
see an impetuous hard-mouthed brute overpower-
ing a weak lad and rushing at stiff timber like a
bull at a gate. This much at least will scarcely
be gainsaid, our horses (to say nothing of their

riders) seldom last long at cross-country work. The continual hard raps on heavy redgum or stringy bark rails, coupled with the constant jarring shocks caused by landing on a soil baked by an Australian sun, is enough to cripple the strongest knees and wear out the toughest sinews in a very few seasons. I have nothing perhaps to suggest that can claim the merit of originality —for has not " The General " already called public attention to these matters ?—but if the scale of our cross-country handicaps was raised till the weights ranged say from 12st. 12lbs. or 12st. 10lbs., to 9st. 10lbs., I think we should get a better and more respectable class of riders, for there are gentlemen here that would ride their own horses if they could ; and should the pace be a little slower, the race would be at least equally well contested : also, if steeplechasing were contested at a proper time of the year, when the ground is springy and yielding or even heavy and sloppy, the advantages to horse and man are too obvious to need any comment. I should be sorry to see the impediments of a fair hunting country transformed into a series of wretched little obstructions that a donkey could surmount, and I do not dislike stiff timber more than some of my neighbours do. A few big posts and rails are almost indispensable, as no other fence neces-

sitates such clean jumping ; and besides, these are
the obstacles most frequently met with in this
country. But a steeplechase would be prettier to
look at, and pleasanter as well as easier to the
ordinary run of competitors, biped as well as
quadruped, if the line were varied a little, and
interspersed with a few green hedges of gorse and
acacia nicely clipped and trimmed, a wattle fence
or two, and a stake and bound, besides a sprink-
ling of palings and walls, and a water-jump made
to resemble a brook, with room for at least half a
dozen horses to take it abreast, and not an impossible cross between a mud-hole and a man-trap
stuck in the middle of a crowd. Alterations such
as these might be made on a few of our principal
courses with comparatively little expense, and
would probably be found to give satisfaction. It
may be objected that stiff timber is the orthodox
hunting leap in these colonies, but in the hunting-
field there are plenty of soft places to be found,
and brush fences and small log jumps are common
enough ; besides all this, a man riding to hounds
can always get a pull at awkward places, whereas,
in a steeplechase, anything like a steady pull is
the exception. Under the present system it is no
wonder that our jumping horses are either crippled
or cowed prematurely, for we usually find that if
their legs last long enough their tempers are

ruined, and they take to baulking with even the best men on their backs, which, considering the way in which they have been handled and schooled from the first, ought not to surprise us.

To nearly all horses timidity is natural, whereas courage is acquired. The horse may be taught by degrees to face things strange and hostile, till from the force of habit he will encounter real dangers willingly and even eagerly, but it is more than doubtful whether he is conscious of the danger he incurs. Thus, whether he is educated for war or for the chase, the chief thing to be instilled is confidence, which can only be acquired by a course of instruction, in which injury to the pupil is avoided as much as possible.

Equine hardihood and fearlessness have been often extolled and exaggerated by romancers and poets, but unless maddened by terror or pain, no horse will willingly rush on a danger that is palpable and self-evident to brute instinct, and even poets and romancers will sometimes bear this in mind. Before the Knight of Rhodes went forth to encounter the dragon, he constructed an effigy of the monster, which he trained his charger to face ; and the quaint old legend actually assumes an air of truth when it tells us

> " Albeit, when first the destrier eyed
> The laidly thing, he swerved aside."

Also (if we rightly remember) in spite of these precautions, the soldier was either unhorsed or compelled to dismount in the actual combat with his serpentine foe.

The story of Quintus Curtius, who rode down the gulf in the Roman Forum, is rather hard to swallow, and Kingsley's spirited ballad, "The Knight's Leap at Altenahr," is somewhat marred by a savour of extreme improbability, unless the old horse that carried the beleaguered freelance "out over the cliff, out into the night," was blind-fold for the occasion.

Far more worthy of credence is the fate of Sir Guy of Linteged and his bride. Without any great stretch of imagination we can fancy the red roan being coaxed to the summit of the tower, and then mounted and backed by main force off the narrow roof that scarcely afforded foothold.

> " Back, he rein'd the steed, back thrown
>   On the slippery coping stone."
>   (Toll slowly.)

> " Back the iron hoofs did grind
>   On the battlements behind
>   Whence a hundred feet went down !"

But to turn from fables to facts. The escape of the only Mameluke that survived Mahomed Ali's treacherous massacre is only one instance among the many that may be cited of desperate feats actually performed on horseback.   There may be men living in India at this moment who remember a certain officer of irregular cavalry; this man, furnished with a common boar spear and a sharp sabre, but with no firearms, and mounted on his favourite horse (probably not a pure Arab, but one of the purest of that breed that could be obtained in Hindostan), used to kill tigers single-handed on open ground.

As far as knowledge founded upon hearsay and not upon actual experience goes, it is to the Arab pure and unadulterated that we award the palm for courage and intelligence, and yet it seems strange that our second-rate horses are prized and our third-rate ones tolerated in India, where Arabian blood ought to be easily procured.

In these rambling remarks, which must now be brought to a close, I have perhaps said enough to express my own opinion, that horse-racing, in spite of its many abuses, is useful, not so much for its own immediate sake as a national pastime, as for the benefits which it must indirectly confer upon our horse stock. Surely for this reason alone it is worth our while to assist the turf in encouraging a really useful class of horse, and in doing justice to the same. Perhaps there are few spots on the earth more favoured by nature for the breeding of horses than Australia. The bright mellow climate, the rich and spacious pasture lands, and the large tracts of fertile soil where every kind of horse fodder can be grown to perfection, all conduce to this end. Nearly every Australian can ride more or less; in the bush there are men who spend half their lives in the saddle, and the townsmen are mostly fond of horse exercise ; and this is as it should be, for a bracing gallop round the suburbs before or after business hours is better than billiards and Bourke Street.

It looks like a remote contingency now, but sooner or later Australia, like every other nation, may have to fight for her own land, and in a country so favourable for cavalry operations a few squadrons of mounted riflemen, supported by horse artillery, ought to do good execution among any invaders that may have effected a landing : and one of our national sports, now as heretofore tarnished and brought to blame, may play no inconsiderable part in increasing our national resources and strengthening our national defences.

THE RING AND THE BOOKS.

THERE is not much in a name, perhaps, but I prefer a good one when it costs nothing, and the palpable plagiarism of my title will hardly attract the notice of those by whom my article will be read, since the story of Pompilia is probably a sealed book to them, and a ring into which they care not to intrude.

There are sundry and divers rings; there are rings lawful and rings contrary to the law, but the betting ring is neither the one nor the other. A bet is not recoverable in a court of law—though there has been, I believe, an exception even to this rule—but in a land of law and order the betting-ring is a recognized institution, and though the authorities of a lawful pastime are supposed to ignore bets, they never fail to take cognisance of known defaultership; the bookmakers print and circulate the odds they offer; lists containing the current prices are posted in places of public resort; the sporting press publishes the state of the turf market, and the subscription betting-room is duly swept and garnished.

The ring is a parasite of the turf, distinct from, and yet amalgamating with the same, and though betting is no part or parcel of our national sports, yet it clings to these, and more especially to the turf: firstly, because horse-racing is legal, and can be worked upon openly; secondly, because it is popular, and can be worked upon largely; thirdly, because, from its very nature, it affords more room for speculation than any other game.

Betting is frequently confounded with gambling; but, strictly speaking, betting is not gambling. You back a certain horse for a certain race, and it is to be assumed that you have, or think you have, some knowledge of that horse's capabilities against probable competitors over a given distance, under a known or a likely weight. You speculate, in short, on the probable performance of the animal, using your judgment in a speculation which is a question of equine speed and bottom, backed by human forethought and skill. Of course there are some risks and chances which you accept willingly and incur by premeditation, but every speculation involves more or less risk. Merchants, squatters, dealers, all speculate; and every monetary transaction is a speculation. You may put your money into the bank; the bank may break to-morrow, but you speculate on the chance of the bank not breaking. A pure gambler speculates on luck without judgment in a question of pure chance. An acquaintance of mine backed Mr. G.'s nomination for the Cup. In so doing he took a liberty with the property of a man whom he barely knows by sight. He would be taking a most unwarrantable liberty if he were to ask Mr. G. to pay up for or to start the horse in order to suit him. A backer of horses may be intensely disgusted if he finds that he has invested upon a horse not meant for the race, but he has no right to be disgusted with any one but himself. It is a self-evident fact that if a man backs a horse belonging to a stranger, he increases the risks against himself and in the bookmaker's favour, risks and chances to which they (the bookmakers) are fairly entitled. As to the old stale claptrap about racehorses being " the property of the public," we know that no sensible racing man nowadays runs horses to suit the public. Some Quixotic nobleman may have done such a thing once or twice in England against his own judgment and inclination, and some idiot may have called him a good sportsman for doing so; but if, as is likely enough, the horse was unfit or amiss in any way, he did an unsportsmanlike and unhorsemanlike thing in racing him. A good sportsman is not of necessity a good horseman, but he is always a good horse-master.

And the public in these cases is simply the betting public—a very insignificant portion of the general public, numerically small, and collectively not by any means select. Bookmakers, backers of horses, and ring men of all classes, arrogate to themselves the prerogatives of the public, and say, " You should run your horses to suit our books ; " but these men know—none better—that owners and trainers of horses have no sympathy with them, nor with each other.

A racing man is, in his vocation, an Ishmaelite, his hand against every man's, and every man's hand against his. The pastime of the real public is the business of the racing public, and to every racing man it is a battle in which he must excel, outwit, or outmanœuvre his fellows to succeed at all. There are no Eglintons or Exeters in this country (and very few at home, now, for that matter), and the folly that expects a racing man to inconvenience himself for his rivals is about on a par with the stupidity that confounds the cry of a few betting men with the *vox populi*.

I am well aware that some of these remarks will not be considered strictly orthodox. I am fully prepared to admit that this system of out-witting and outmanœuvring gives birth to grave offences. I will not attempt to deny that the ring exercises in many ways an evil influence over the

turf (though I doubt whether that influence is one
of unmitigated evil). I know, moreover, that
offences against turf law are either clumsily con-
trived and carelessly carried out, or else that they
are undiscovered, and consequently unpunished.
I also know that a 'cute turf lawyer can steer very
close to the wind, and outride the squalls of turf
jurisdiction and the seas of public opinion ; and I
still maintain that racehorses cannot and will not
run to suit or to satisfy the public.

As a literary freelance, hovering between the
borders of the turf and the confines of the fourth
estate, I speak of things as I believe them to be—
not as others think they ought to be. I should
perhaps write differently if I wrote a leading
article instead of a fugitive waif. I should then
consider the conservative character of the press
and advocate the possible adoption of that high
honourable standard which the press sets up as a
model for every turfite. "'Tis a consummation
most devoutly," &c., but I fear it won't come to
pass in our time. I have a great respect for
"The Press," with good reason. The press is
sometimes pompous, the press is often prosy, but
the press is always respectable. The press has
the interests of the turf at heart, though the press
may err with the best intentions. Infallible in the
abstract, erroneous enough in the concrete, the

press, though choked with straining at gnats and gorged with swallowing camels, survives the labour and the repletion—blundering ever, yet ever bearing for its motto, " Fair as the moon, clear as the sun, terrible as an army with banners," or something equally sublime and ridiculous.

Every horse and man on the turf is the property of the public in one way—he is the property of the press, and can be taken to task at any time. Unfortunately, the horses care very little what the press says, and the men, after being hauled over the coals once or twice, care just as little. It is startling for the first time to see your name in print, coupled with a vague censorious innuendo, or a mysterious uncomplimentary insinuation, but, "bless you, it's nothing when you're used to it." " My dear fellow, I'm sorry to have to slate you—from long practice I can steer as close to a libel as you can to a turf statute ; but I sha'n't really hurt you, and your friends will think none the worse of you for what I say. Let the scribe earn his column conscientiously."

We may abuse the ring to our heart's content, but call it by what name we will—a parasite, a spurious offshoot, a morbid growth, a diseased excrescence—the ring is inseparable from the turf. More than this. If the death-blow of the turf were dealt to-morrow, all the gambling element of the ring would survive it, and would break out in twenty different places, like the heads of the hydra—

" Quique redundabat fœcundo vulnere serpens."

Possibly we might abolish horse-racing, though the same is very doubtful, for even if we were "virtuous"—which we ain't by long chalks—the supply of cakes and ale would not be materially diminished—but we could never put a stop to gambling, and whether good or evil preponderates in the mixture of sport and speculation that constitutes the turf, it would be somewhat hard to decide. In far higher and graver walks of life we sometimes see the two elements blended as grotesquely as in that oddly assorted pair that travelled in company to Rome and terrified his Holiness into confession, when

" The beads of the bishop were hanging before,
    And the tail of the devil behind."

On the average, I fear, the caudal appendage of the Prince of Darkness outweighs and outreaches the rosary.

Let me conclude with a few remarks on books and bookmakers. Bookmakers, of course, are fair game ; they are the scapegoats of the turf. There are two types of the conventional bookmaker of

the novel or the stage—the Jew and the Greek,
the corpulent and the cadaverous, the pursy
Belphegor and Mammon the meagre. You may
see one or the other of them in every modern
sporting tale, so I shall not describe them. But
the real live bookmaker is quite a different article.
I think our bookmakers, for instance, are, in the
main, rather a fair average lot; if no better than
our sporting men of other classes—owners of
horses, trainers, backers, and jocks—they are
certainly no worse. With their private lives I
have nothing to do, nor with their occupations
outside the turf. I should certainly prefer to do
business with one or two that I know: but if I
were a betting man, and could get a point longer
odds from another party, I should not inquire into
his moral character; he might preside over
chambers where you may see closed doors, drawn
blinds, and burning lamps by day, while in the
dusk of the innermost fane the mysteries of poker
or Yankee grab are celebrated. Or he may act as
master of the revels,

> "Where Pan by noon and Bacchus by night,
> Fleeter of foot than the fleet-foot kid,
> Follows with dancing and fills with delight
> The Mænad and the Bassarid."

*C'est bizarre sans doute mais ce n'est pas mon
affaire.*

We are not censorious nowadays. We prefer to live in charity with all men—Jews, Turks, infidels, and heretics included.

It is the fashion at present to regard their vagaries with faint cynical amusement—nothing more. If we happen by any chance to meet some one rather worse than ourselves, we feel better by comparison and more charitable ; and on the turf all men are equal, as long as they pay. Is this a bad sign ? I don't know. Some say the turf is going down hill very fast, and some say the ring is at the bottom of this decline. I don't believe it. Fifty years ago things were no better, and it was much the same five centuries back, I fancy.

The knights of our ring are no worse than the champions of that ancient circular absurdity yclept " The Round Table." They were stronger in those days—more biceps and better digestions. They drank mead instead of P.B., and they had no tobacco, but in other respects their morals were nothing to boast of—

> " What time among King Arthur's crew
> 　Thereof came jeer and laugh,
> One knight—true mate of lady true—
> 　Alone the cup could quaff."

I suppose Lancelot would have been about first favourite for that event if he had gone for the sugar. I wonder if he was made safe. "Both Reged wide and fair Strathclyde and Carlisle tower and town" was a stake worth winning, to say nothing of the Pendragon, and he might have pulled off the double event and squared Guinivere. I daresay the bookmakers got at him. Perhaps you never read the story; it is rather good, but the moral is obscure.

THE old question of Arab blood as a means of regenerating our horse-stock has been revived by Mr. Upton's letter, a copy of which appears in the *Australasian.* If discussion were at all likely to beget action in a matter of such importance to our breeders and to all men of equestrian pursuits, it would be worth our while to promote debate, and even to promote controversy, both as to the probable advantages to be derived from an Arab strain, and also as to the possible means of procuring that strain unadulterated.

I think most men will agree with me when I state my conviction that the English horse is too matured, even in these colonies, to reap much benefit from an infusion of impure blood with an Arab cross; and the difficulty of procuring an Arab of stainless pedigree must be very great, yet if such a thing exists it can be surmounted.

In India, which is not so very far from Arabia, there are no Arabs of very high caste; if it were otherwise, our third-rate planters would not be thought so much of in India—that is, supposing the pure Arab to be as good as he is represented. Nor can the Arab proper be found in parts of the East much nearer his birthplace. The Persian horse is a pretty mongrel, the Turkoman a degenerate hybrid, and the Barb a hardy bastard. The Pasha of Egypt, probably, has no clean-bred Arab in his stables. Some of your readers may remember in 1850 or 1851 (I am not sure of the date) that potentate actually sent a challenge to the English Jockey Club offering to run any English horse ten miles. The match never came off, for obvious reasons, yet not very long ago a little Irish huntress called " Fair Nell " (or some such name) made an example of the best Egyptian Arabs. I do not recall this circumstance to the discredit of the real Arab, though I have no scruples about disparaging the half-bred one. I am ready enough to believe, with many other believers, that nearly all over the world the saddle-horse owes what speed and stamina he may possess to his Arabian forefathers, from the Tartar of the Ukraine to the Mustang of the pampas and prairies, that carried to Columbia, with the cavalry of Cortez, some homœopathic dose of Arab blood, originally transmitted to Spain by the Moors of Barbary ; and yet, in spite of this belief, none of us have seen anything equal to our own English blood-horse, and the Arab refuses to leave the region of sand and simoom to confirm our faith or to gratify our curiosity, and we cannot quite extinguish a lurking doubt that will intrude occasionally. This blind faith in the unseen Arab may be a prejudice engendered by traditionary romance, and fostered by the exaggerated stories of enthusiastic travellers —incompetent, or at least impractical judges of horseflesh as a rule. This desert-born courser, whose speed is unapproachable, whose courage is unrivalled, whose symmetry is faultless, and whose lineage laughs to scorn the proudest pedigree in our stud-book, may be a visionary creation of the brain. Our ideal Arab may have no real existence outside " the Book of Job." If ever he did exist, he may be extinct and obsolete. He may have followed the tracks of pre-Adamite saurians, or he may be a myth, a hippogriff, a unicorn, or a fable from beginning to end.

" Palgrave " has certainly written well and sensibly on this subject, but with all due deference to " Palgrave " as an accomplished scholar and a clever scribe, he may be a theoretical rather than a practical judge of horses. . Perhaps in the whole stud of Nedjid there is nothing that can extend the winner of last year's Derby—perhaps no Scheik or Emir of Bedouin tribes owns a horse that can live for twenty months over grass with a weight-carrying hunter of the " Shires,"—perhaps the hardy native pony that carries the lean, swart Ishmaelite of the present day may be esteemed by his master, because, as a specimen of the animal kingdom, he is rather superior to the unwashed ophthalmia-stricken semi-savage that bestrides him.

I do not seek to propagate these views. I do not even give them as my own, but doubts of this kind may probably have led many besides myself to speculate in like manner. For my own part, I confess a weakness for the old prejudice, and a regard for the old romance. It may have been the Arab horse that made the green-turbaned squadrons irresistible in the days when "the prophet who preached by the sword" led his wild disciples conquering and to conquer. The steeds that devoured the desert before them, when "the red cross" fled in company with the crescent, may have left a progeny whose excellences may have been handed down as heirlooms to posterity through a long line of undegenerated descendants, and some few drops of that blood may have found their way through the veins of the Darley or Godolphin into the English stud-book, "which fully accounts, gentlemen," &c. All these things are possible. Q. Are they probable?

"Fortes creantur fortibus et bonis."
(" Ponies that are good, breed good and useful ponies.")

But facts are stubborn things, and there are some few questions which may puzzle the advocate of the Arab. For if the Darley Arabian was clean bred, we can get a clean-bred Arab now as we could in the days of Darley. The demand is greater now than it was then, and the means of obtaining the article demanded are surely more facile.

How is it, then, that all the Arabs purchased, presented, or otherwise exported and imported from the East to Europe, are now found to compare unfavourably with the English thoroughbred? "These are not pure Arabs," says the special pleader of the equine Ishmaelite; but some of these ought to be as pure as the Darley, or nearly so—as pure as the Byerly Turk, at all events, for he was only a cocktail Arab, and yet some of his descendants did well on English soil—witness the Flying Dutchman.

If, on the other hand, as is very generally believed, neither the Turk aforesaid, nor the Godolphin, nor even the Darley, was equally pure, then the superiority of our blood-horses is probably owing to the care and cultivation that has been lavished on them in breeding, rearing, and training, rather than to that small infusion of Arabian blood which has found its way into their veins. When the Moors held the south of Spain they rode Barbs, some of which were probably three-parts Arab; and when

Boabdil el Zohra had to evacuate Granada, he and his followers left behind a great many of these Barbs and Arabs. Even now the Spanish horse, especially the Andalusian, shows a great deal of the Arab breed. As far north as Limousin there are still traces of the boasted blood, but what good has it done, so far as improving the breed goes? The Spanish jennet is a showy, useless nondescript, and though the French light cavalry used to get some fairish mounts from Limousin, they never rode anything that we should call second class.

I believe that the English thoroughbred is of mixed breed, and some fortunate nick or dovetail may have done much to make him what he is, but his superiority is to a great extent owing to artificial means—*i.e.*, training and attention. Strength and endurance are sometimes (not always) hereditary, but average merit in strength, speed, or endurance will, with patience and proper training, develop into surpassing excellence. Why not? Even courage is often an acquired thing. Harry of Navarre is only one historical instance of the fact that the child's text copy—" Familiarity breeds contempt "—applies to dangers as well as to other matters.

The turf with all its abuses, and the chase with all its offences (against farmers), have done more probably towards the improvement of our horse-

stock than an accidental importation of a pony
with a mysterious pedigree, whose ancestor may
have borne one of the dukes of Edom, or worked
as near-side leader in Pharaoh's chariot, or carried
an outrider in the train of the Queen of Sheba.

As for the cry now raised about the degeneracy
of our thoroughbred, I have heard the same nearly
a score of years ago. I have heard it often
since. In fact, it is a periodical cry, but a very
slight cause may raise it a little earlier, or make
it a little louder than usual. Mr. Upton says,
"The state of the English horse is not what it
should be, because few are satisfied with him."
Few are satisfied, indeed, because competition is
so great, and every man wants to breed, train, or
ride something exceptionally good—better, in fact,
than anything in his neighbourhood. If it were
otherwise, and men were satisfied, we should have
stagnation in place of competition; and breeding
would go to the mischief and horses to the dogs.
Of course, when some ill-starred trainer cannot
successfully compete with his more successful
rival, it is the material he works upon that is at
fault. When some unlucky or unskilled rider cannot cut down like grass a better or bolder man, the
degenerate quadruped comes in for the blame, in
that the merest trifle will start the old refrain,
"Our horses have degenerated." "I could ride a

better horse ten years ago," says Mr. ——, who is reckoned a high authority, because he is a fair judge of horses, and really could ride once. If he were to say, " I could ride a better horse when I was ten years younger," he would be nearer the truth. There are more horses of all classes now, and consequently more bad ones. If there are fewer stars it is because the fields are harder to beat, which is a good sign. I fancy there is not much difference between the cracks of fifteen or sixteen years ago and those of the present day, but what difference there is seems to be in our favour. The Flying Dutchman was a good horse, so was West Australian, but Blair Athol was probably as good as the worst of these, and Gladiateur certainly better than either. If we go back to the traditions of Flying Childers we have no criterion. Childers was the only racehorse of his. day—a Triton among minnows ; and the same may be said of Eclipse, who could distance the best horse that could be brought against him. Of these two, Childers is Mr. Upton's favourite, because he assumes that the Darley was a purer Arabian than Godolphin, and prefers him accordingly ; but we know very little about Childers except that he was the best of a bad lot, and that there was a legend, utterly void of foundation, and believed by no rational being, about some extraordinary time that he did a mile in. In truth, those were barbarous times, and stop-watches were probably not very reliable. Fancy a race-horse with a short square dock! I wonder that they didn't clip his ears like those of a fighting dog. Mr. Upton's letter is a theme for speculative interest rather than a page of interesting information. I do not think he has even made the most of his case; his data are sometimes erroneous, and his reasoning occasionally illogical. I remember both Teddington and Daniel O'Rourke; and I don't believe either of these could be called " a small, powerful horse." Sir Joseph's chestnut was light and almost weedy-looking, with a straight shoulder and small arms and gaskins. He was a rare goer, certainly; to say nothing of his Derby, in which he beat a bad field almost in a walk; his performance in the Cups at Goodwood, Doncaster, and Ascot have stamped him as a flyer of the highest flight. Daniel, on the other hand, was an ordinary pony enough, in the Derby a rank outsider. Barbarian, not mentioned in the betting, ran him to half a neck or a head, and ought to have beaten him, and there was a good third close up, whose name no one had heard before, and every one has forgotten since. If Stockwell and Kingston were in the ruck, it simply proves that they were no good on that day; and as a stallion, how could Daniel compare with the sire of Rataplan? Mr. Upton has a weakness for "little big horses," because the Arabs are supposed to be undersized, but he is not good in his illustrations of good little big ones.

But I do not wish to cavil at Mr. Upton's letter, and I am willing enough to believe that the main argument is right. Our horses have not improved very fast, and duffers still predominate. An infusion of fresh Arab blood would certainly do no harm, and might possibly work wonders. If we could only go back to the fountain-head, and pick the most perfect Arab of the purest strains, we should probably be more or less successful. The thing is worth a trial anyhow; we will take this at least for granted. The next question is catching your Arab.

But I must wind up abruptly, having trespassed too long. Go to Arabia and introduce yourself to the Sultan of Nedjid, and make presents to his stud-groom, if he has one, and look over his stables carefully, and make your selection, choosing the best horses, and buy at any price if the Sultan will sell; and if he won't, which is likely enough, you have still one chance.

Settle down in the desert for a year or two at least, and try your luck with the nomadic chiefs, for some of these have horses equal to the Sultan's;

but they are hard to deal with, and though the better class of them are not very bad, and are hospitable enough, they would think nothing of taking the life of a Christian dog; and besides, they are half robbers by trade. However, if you are a good Arabic scholar, and have the Koran at your fingers' ends, and know the Romance of Antâr by heart, and can recite and tell stories, and make yourself agreeable; and if you can reconcile yourself to the manners and customs of the Bedouins (their manners are none, for that matter, and their customs are filthy); and if you can live on a draught of camel's milk or a handful of barley or rice, with a few dates, perhaps; and if you can put up with dust and drought and vermin; and if you have tact and coolness, and confidence and presence of mind, you will get on well enough. And then, if you are a good horseman, and can use weapons of war, and would not mind taking your chance in an occasional skirmish, and would have no objection to espouse the favourite daughter of some vagabond Scheik, and no scruples against embracing the Mahometan faith, which is simple, primitive and Mosaic, you may possibly get a genuine Arabian horse as dower or heirloom, or even as a captive of your bow and your spear; and if you escape fevers, and plagues, and sand-storms, and sabre cuts, and shots and stabs, and such-like trifling contingencies, and make your escape with your prize, and get clear away, and come anywhere within my reach, I will certainly, with your permission, come to see this pearl of great price, and wish you luck with him.

POLITICAL SPEECHES.

REFERENCE has been made in the Memoir to Gordon's political career, and I propose giving in the following pages a brief record of that period of his life which, to the poet himself, must have appeared just as inharmonious with his tastes and inclinations as it does to his loving admirers of the present day. Very little has hitherto been said of Gordon's Parliamentary work, and no effort has been made to rescue his speeches from the limbo of old newspaper files or unread *Hansards*. These speeches are specially interesting as affording a still clearer view of the character of this remarkable and most unfortunate man.

Moreover the cry has been raised: "Give us all Gordon has written or spoken;" and it is to meet this want, growing out of the deep affection of the people for the "brave great soul that never told a lie, or turned aside to fly from danger," that I have been prompted to insert all the speeches he made in Parliament, including his chief "hustings" speech delivered before a public meeting held at Mount Gambier on Jan. 18, 1865.

This meeting was called in order to give the various candidates an opportunity of expounding their political views. Dr. Wehl occupied the chair, and Gordon was introduced to the meeting by Mr. Burton as a "suitable candidate, and hoped the electors would give him a favourable hearing."

"Mr. Gordon said—At the meeting on that day week he had promised to address them and give them his opinions on the leading political questions of the day. He had been asked if he were favourable to leasing the land in hundreds in small blocks. He was not. Those who had bought land in the hundreds had a certain vested right in the unsold portion, and Government would not be justified in taking away that right. Besides, it would not be wise on the part of the Government to lock up the land to purchasers by leasing it in small blocks. (Hear, hear.) As to free distillation, as such a measure, if carried, would involve the necessity of the removal of the import duty upon spirits, and so decrease the revenue, he was opposed to it. Government, he thought, wisely raised a large revenue from spirits. It was a tax that was paid by the wealthy and those who could well afford it. If the revenue ever became so large that the country could dispense with any part of it, he should prefer to lighten the taxes on the necessaries of life. It was said to be a measure for the benefit of the farmer; but so far as this district was concerned he could not see it in that light. It would no doubt be a great boon to the winegrowers, but as this was not a wine-growing district the measure could not benefit it. Besides, the winegrowers did not need any such measure. The Government liberally allowed them the privilege of fortifying their wines with brandy of their own manufacture already. They had, therefore, as large a measure of free distillation as it was wise to confer upon them at present. (Applause.) On the question of immigration, he was opposed to the present system, and unless the Government sanctioned a more equitable distribution of the immigrants on their arrival in the colony he would oppose its continuance. At the present time the labour market of the district was supplied from Melbourne. The immigrants brought out at the general expense were solely for the benefit of Adelaide; and unless the country at large were to reap a share of the benefit he could not see why they should support it. (Cheers.) He was in favour of carrying out the present system of education, and so long as it

did not interfere with religious creeds and parties
he should favour its extension. He was in favour
of increasing the salaries of country teachers.
(Applause.) The mining interest was an important one, and he was sorry it was not one of the
interests of the district. As it was he was
prepared to give such attention to it as would
make it contribute its fair share to the public
revenue. (Cheers.) As to the Northern Territory,
he would not say much about it. But he was
anxious that it should receive such attention as
would ensure its advancement, but he was
opposed to its being a drag upon the colony. He
was in favour of *ad valorem* duties. They were a
most fair way of raising a revenue. In 1860 the
Government repealed the *ad valorem* duty, but they
soon saw their mistake, and it was reimposed in
1863. The idea that its repeal was a great boon
to the poor man was a great fallacy. Wealthy
squatters and merchants imported their goods
direct, and had them free of duty, thus escaping
the burden of taxation, which fell upon many of
the necessaries of life, and pressed heavily upon
those who were least able to pay it. (Cheers.)
He was in favour of an assimilation of the tariff
of the colony to that of other colonies. He was
also in favour of the Real Property Act. He was
in favour of the Government borrowing money for

reproductive works, such as roads, bridges, jetties, &c. Whatever tended to benefit the colony and develop its resources might properly be regarded as a reproductive work. (Hear, hear.) To borrow money, therefore, for such works as he had mentioned would be the duty of a wise Government. Some people had a horror of a national debt. He had no sympathy with them. He viewed it with no alarm. So long as they had a boundless country, of undeveloped resources to mortgage for the small sum that would be necessary to push it ahead, they were acting on a wrong principle in being so cautious. (Applause.) While on this subject he might say that the Government had been very niggardly with regard to the country districts — particularly with the South-East. (Hear, hear.) The expenditure around Adelaide was unchecked and uncavilled at, while every paltry sum voted for the district was given with the worst possible grace. He might mention the Gaol, for instance—a resolution to erect which was passed three years ago, but it was not yet commenced. In the interim Adelaide had its costly Waterworks, and now they had passed a resolution to erect fine new Houses of Parliament at a cost of £50,000. This he regarded as great extravagance while so much necessary work remained to be done. If returned it would be his

care that the country districts obtained their fair
share of the revenue for public purposes. (Cheers.)
He would support a Road Bill providing for the
making of main lines out of the General Revenue,
but was in favour of a measure that would provide
for the maintenance of those roads by local or
some other mode of taxation. Believing that the
district was inadequately represented by two members, he was in favour of an increase of members.
(Applause.) He was in favour of having a good road
made between MacDonnell Bay and Penola, and
should advocate an immediate inspection and report as to the best mode to do it. He was in favour
of a grant to erect a District Hospital at Mount
Gambier, and he would try without loss of time
to get one. He might mention that Mr. John
Riddoch had promised a very handsome sum for
this work as a supplement to any Government
grant. (Cheers.) As to Goyder's valuations
he looked upon them as a past event. He saw
a notice in the *Gazette* calling upon Crown
lessees to send in written acceptances of Goyder's
valuations, and in the event of their not doing so
the runs would be offered by auction. It was
pretty certain the squatters would accept the
terms imposed upon them. As to whether the
valuations made were right or wrong he could not
say. He knew little about the value of the runs

around Adelaide, and less about those in the Far
North. It would, therefore, be presumptuous in
him to go into detail. But as to the system
pursued, he must say it was grossly unjust. It
was not fair to appoint one man to value all the
runs of the colony. It was a task beyond the
abilities of any one man. In this the Government
had not acted fairly. But their proceedings had
been assented to, and he was willing that the
matter should now rest. It had been asserted
that he was a squatters' advocate. (Hear, hear.)
He was no such thing. He knew but few of the
squatters of the district—he was not the personal
friend of any of them. He had no interest in
squatting property, and he could not tell a
Leicester from a Merino. His squatting
sympathies led him only so far as to wish to see
fair play done. (Applause.) He did not care
whether a man were a squatter or a farmer, he
would feel the same. He would consider that he
ought to have justice. It might, and was argued
by some that the fact of the squatters consenting
to take their runs at the increased valuations was
a sufficient argument as to the justice of them.
It might be justice, but it had a very close resemblance to what was known as " Highland
justice." (Laughter.) The McGregors, the
McAlpines, and the McIvors, when they levied

blackmail from their Lowland neighbours, considered that they were only exacting a just tribute;
but it is needless to say that no amount of taxing
could ever reconcile these neighbours to it, or
make them think otherwise than that " Highland
justice " bore a close resemblance to highway
robbery. (Laughter and cheers.) It was said
that taxing heavily the squatters would benefit the
farmers. He could not see it. He thought it
would injure the farmers, and he could prove so
if there were any necessity. But there was not.
He would invite them to ask him questions, and
he would answer them as far as possible. One
remark he would allude to, made at last week's
meeting. It was proposed that they should bind
the candidates neck and heels to do their bidding.
He did not mean to submit to this process. He
would go into Parliament free and independent if
at all. He would let them know his sentiments
freely, but he reserved to himself the right to
modify them ; and not to please all the electors
on this side of the Equator would he bind himself
down not to do so. He might assure them, however, that he did not change his mind very readily,
and was very conservative of his opinions.
(Applause.)

" In answer to Mr. Wells, Mr. Gordon said he
considered the district inadequately represented by

two members. Mr. Gordon, in answer to Mr.
Harvie, said he was not in favour of good (or bad)
land being surveyed in square-mile blocks, either
around squatters' homesteads or elsewhere. Had
never heard of such being done. Mr. Gordon, in
answer to Mr. Umpherston, said that as immigration was carried on solely for the benefit of
Adelaide, he was opposed to it. Were a more
equitable system of distribution adopted he might
modify his views. This district did not reap
sufficient benefit from the present outlay. In
answer to Mr. Goss, Mr. Gordon said he would
not vote for a Queen's Hundred. He did not think
racing Parliamentary. (Hear, hear.) Though
fond of a little racing personally, he did not think
the country should support it. He thought the
Government ought to support gymnasiums and
kindred sports that promoted the healthy development of the body, more especially in connection
with public schools. (Applause.) In answer to
Mr. Harvie, Mr. Gordon said that all public sales
of land in the district ought to be held in Mount
Gambier. Many had lost good chances from the
system of holding all the land sales in Adelaide.
What little was left ought to be sold at the Mount.
Mr. Gordon, in answer to Mr. Umpherston, said he
was not in favour of substituting the increased land
revenue for the *ad valorem* duty, and doing away

with that tax. He was not in favour of doing away with the Custom-House and taking the land revenue instead for the ordinary purposes of Government. The land revenue ought to be put to the best advantage in developing and advancing the colony. (Applause.) Mr. Gordon, in answer to Mr. Umpherston, said he was not in favour of a land tax for making roads. He did not think it would be requisite to tax the land for that purpose. It had plenty of burdens without additional ones. (Hear, hear.) Mr. Gordon, in answer to Mr. South, said that all public moneys voted for the district and spent in it ought to be accounted for by a balance-sheet published in the local papers. He was not only in favour of that, but he was in favour of the public having a control over it to say how and where it should be spent. It was useless getting grants if they were spent where the public did not want them. Mr. Gordon, in answer to Mr. Shelton, said he would support a Bill for closing public-houses during the whole of the Sabbath, except in the case of bonâ fide travellers. Mr. Gordon, in answer to Mr. Harvie, said that he was in favour of the principle of self-government, and that every place of any importance was entitled to a District Council if it desired one. Mr. Harvie asked if Mr. Gordon would pledge himself to abide by his present opinions, and honestly carry them out. Mr. Gordon said he had no idea of the sort of pledge that was wanted of him, or of the way in which he was to take it. But he had no intention of taking any oath or affidavit in the matter. His word was as good as his bond. He would do the best he could for the district, but if they would not take his word he would not give them any pledge. (Applause.) "

On March 6th following it was announced that " Messrs. Riddoch and Gordon have been returned, Attorney-General Stow having lost by a majority of three." On May 23, 1865, " Mr. Gordon took the oath and his seat for the electoral district of Victoria." On May 31st he spoke as follows on a motion which condemned the Government of the day for its proposal to put up certain annual leases for public competition :—

" Mr. Gordon said it appeared to him that there were two questions to be considered—first, the amount of evil, real or imaginary, which would accrue to the holders of present annual leases ; and secondly, what amount of good, if any, would be reaped by the general public as a set-off to the losses of the lessees. Any person having the most superficial knowledge of pastoral affairs must see that disastrous consequences would fall upon the lessees if compelled to leave the land at a short notice. It was, however, an ill wind that blew nobody good, and perhaps some land-sharks might make a dishonest penny in running up the leases. It was clear to him that neither agriculturist nor merchant, nor any honest class of the community, would profit by the loss entailed on the lessees by the forced sale of their runs. The hon. member Mr. Townsend spoke as if nearly every member of that House came pledged to support Mr. Goyder's valuations. He was not a squatter, and had no interest in squatting; but he was not returned pledged to support Goyder's valuations. In fact, he told his constituents in language not strictly Parliamentary—(a laugh)—that he would not support Goyder's valuations. He believed that in many respects the squatters had only themselves to blame; and in the question of valuations especially, if they had any grievance to complain of, it arose out of their own consent to accept the valuations of one individual. (Hear, hear.) He might say that he knew plenty of places where 240 sheep were calculated to the square mile which could perhaps fairly carry from 40 to 80 head. They had heard of a gentleman in advance of his time who had recently been charged with lunacy. He thought that the squatters might with equal justice have been taken up on the same charge. He thought there could be no advantage in sacrificing the squatters, and no man could fail to see the hardship that must accrue to many of them if their runs were put up to auction as proposed. If any class could be shown to derive a benefit, perhaps they would not complain; but it would be folly to throw the squatters overboard if nobody was to be a gainer. He was disposed to support the motion."

On June 6th he returned to the question, and delivered the following intensely characteristic speech :—

"Mr. Speaker—Sir—Last week the Government and this honourable House after a long discussion and a great deal of speechifying—good, bad, and indifferent — passed a resolution in favour of an amendment of the hon. member for East Adelaide, which amendment I had the honour of supporting; and I may here observe that upon the occasion to which I allude I came into the House prepared to support the motion of the hon. member for the Port, but it was proved to me that if the motion was good the amendment was something better. I cannot understand the policy which would cast a resolution one day and the next day knock it upon the head. It looks to me like labour in vain, and calls to mind the legend in the Greek mythology, where Sisyphus is engaged in continually rolling a stone up a hill—an employment in itself probably agreeable, but decidedly monotonous — (a laugh) — or like the snail in the schoolboy's problem, which goes up the hill two inches by day and falls back one inch every night ; but there at least some progress is made. Our motto is 'Advance'—'*Vestigia nulla retrorsum*' —and shall we emulate that renowned commander who with 20,000 men marched up a hill and then marched down again ? You may talk about Goyder's valuations, annual leases, &c., from noon till dark, and it's a matter of sublime indifference to me personally whether 'Trojan or Tyrian' squatter or anti-squatter gain the ascendency. Now they tell me that the squatters must go to the wall. Well, it won't hurt me, that's one comfort ; and perhaps, who knows, in those halcyon days to which the hon. Treasurer tells us we may now look forward, when the *ad valorem* taxes are repealed, when the blessings of free distillation are reaped by the public in general and by the teetotalers in particular, when railways and suchlike Utopian luxuries flourish in the South-Eastern Scrub—in short, when we enjoy a sort of colonial millennium—who knows, I say, but that some of us in the fulness of our hearts may devise some scheme to shorten the period of rebuke and blasphemy to which we have been justly doomed—the condemned class, the *enfants perdus*, the *morituri*, the squatters. I often wonder how it is that so

few persons can divest themselves altogether of
prejudice and party spirit and take a calm and
dispassionate view of the squatting question. The
two opposite factions stand opposed to each other
like Scylla and Charybdis of old, and it seems that
all the passers-by must be drawn irresistibly into
the vortex of the one or on to the rocks of the
other. I quite agree with the hon. member who
stated that no man ought to have one line of
policy for the hustings and another for the House;
but I think that a distinction may well be drawn
between promises made to conciliate favour, which
ought to be binding, and opinions expressed carelessly in open defiance, which may upon mature
reflection be somewhat modified. Thus, if in the
late election I betrayed any extreme views on the
squatting side, I was then actuated chiefly by
antipathy to those prejudices which our op-
ponents worked so ably. The blind egotism
of a set of illiterate boors, and the senseless
clamour of the great unwashed—the *canaille*, as
the French call them — was alone enough to
aggravate a saint into a spirit of contradiction.
I now wish to treat this case fairly and impar-
tially, whatever I may have done. There can
be no doubt but that the squatters have long held
the Crown lands at a nominal rent. Like their
own stock they have fattened on the broad pas-

tures of the colony until some of them may
possibly have begun to fancy that they ought to
be left in perpetual possession of those happy
hunting-grounds, where for so many years they
have held undisputed sway, smoked the calumet
of peace, and enjoyed their *otium cum dignitate*
undisturbed by the encroachments of strangers.
Goyder's valuations gave them a gentle reminder
that such was not the case, and they saw pretty
plainly that some of the gilt was to be taken off
their gingerbread.   But the outcry which was
raised by the settlers and their parasites against
the Government and the new valuations was surely
no worse than the furious onslaughts which have
been made from time to time upon them by the
opposite faction.   Besides, there was more reason
in this outcry than some of you may be aware of;
for had these valuations been carried out in the
full rigour with which they were first proposed,
there would have been some cause for complaint,
and surely the squatters were right in crying out
before they were hurt.   There would clearly have
been no use in making a fuss after the mischief
was done.   I do not object to Goyder's valuations
on account of their severity, because I believe that
in most cases the lessees of the Crown have been
dealt with leniently enough ; but I do not see how
any one man can have done the work supposed to

be done by Goyder in the given time. There are
in the South-East many runs, on the carrying
capabilities of which no man could form a correct
estimate unless he visited them at two distinct
seasons of the year. In the winter perhaps two-
thirds of them are under water. Again, in some
districts there are large tracts of country which
look fair enough to the eye, but which at the same
time are so unhealthy, so tainted with coast
disease, that sheep and even cattle will only live
there at certain periods of the year. And then,
again, the burden of these valuations will not in
my opinion be equally distributed. There are
some second and third-class runs which have
been very highly improved. The tenants—hard-
working, industrious men — have toiled and
expended their profits in erecting substantial
buildings, woolsheds, and dwelling-houses, divided
the runs with stone walls and sheep-proof fences,
dug drains, &c. Now, if these runs were sur-
rendered by the tenants and resumed by the
Government, these improvements would be for-
feited; thus these lessees of the Crown are
compelled to accept the valuations or lose
everything. It is absurd to say that no case of
hardship has occurred. A run was sold not long
ago near Mount Gambier; it must have been
forced into the market by pressure of circum-

stances, or it would not have been sent to the hammer at such an unfavourable time. With stock and improvements it was honestly worth £20,000, but it fetched not quite half that sum. You may say that it was not the Valuator which did this? No, but it was the panic caused by these valuations, and it amounts to the same thing. I believe that man was ruined. But, as I said before, I do not find fault with the severity of Goyder's valuations. On the average, I do not consider them severe, neither do I condemn them on account of one or two isolated cases of hardship. Perhaps no great change ever took place in any country where the mass was benefited without there being a few sufferers. I have great confidence in Mr. Goyder, and I believe that he has done all that one man could do to give satisfaction to the Government, and also, as far as lay in his power, to deal fairly with the squatters. But what was his task? He had to travel all over the colony to visit all the runs, to ascertain, by personal inspection, the carrying capabilities of those runs, and to report accordingly, and all within a few weeks. Sir, I must affirm that the most laborious of the labours of Hercules—which I take to be the cleansing of the Augean Stables—was child's play compared to this. There is another grievance which is so palpable that I cannot help alluding to it, though it affects the agriculturist, and, in fact, every class of landowner, as much as it does the squatter. I allude to the depasturing licences. Under the increased Assessment Act those landowners who wish to make use of the hundreds have to pay 8d. per head for sheep and 4s. per head for cattle. This soon makes up a considerable sum, which, when paid, entitles him to a right of commonage for one twelvemonth ; but perhaps the next month these lands are surveyed and put up to auction, and whether he buys himself, or whether his neighbour buys, he gets no compensation for a year's rent actually paid in advance. This is a dead loss. As for these annual leases, either the squatters have been very careless, or else there must be some mistake somewhere—something vague and insecure about the terms of the leases, or the lessees would never have been taken by surprise as they have been. It is useless saying the squatters knew that their leases would be thus resumed, and that they should have been prepared. It is useless, because it is simply untrue. The squatters did not know anything of the kind. They knew that their leases might be resumed for sale, but they did not know that they would be resumed to be relet. True, there was some talk about cutting up the runs and reletting them, but it was only talk. On the other hand, it is absurd of the squatters to say that the course which the Government may pursue is not legal, because whatever the Government does must be legal. If not, the Government can pass an Act to make it legal. Sir, the Government may confiscate your property or mine, and make that legal by an Act. They can give as a reason that we have had it long enough ; or, better still, they may give no reason at all. They make it law, and if law I presume it is justice ; but I'll be hanged if they can make you or I call it justice—at least they would not make me. But the old objection has not been got over yet. *Cui bono ?* To whom is it a benefit if the Government inflict an injury on any body of men without conferring an equivalent benefit on another class ? There may be justice in the act, but there is no mercy and very little wisdom. Well, sir, perhaps the squatters do not ask justice, but they want a little mercy by way of a change. Too much of a good thing is bad ; and though justice is a very good thing, yet with the imperfect state of our natures, faith, we may all have enough of it. In conclusion I shall merely state that I think the squatters should contribute a fair share towards the General Revenue, or relinquish their land in favour of public competition. They have had their day, and they ought to have made hay while the sun was shining; probably many of them have, but I do not think that that is any reason for oppressing them heedlessly and wantonly. I do not think they ought to be harassed and hampered in every conceivable way. I do not think that we ought to declare war upon them, and treat them as if they were public enemies. I appeal confidently to a number of intelligent and upright gentlemen. This quarrel is not one of extermination. This is not war to the knife; but the struggle has lasted long enough, has engendered a great deal of ill-feeling, has grown wearisome and tedious; and I think it is time to put an end to it. The attacks and reprisals, the mutual recriminations, the bitter invective, and coarse personal abuse that passed on both sides is enough to make a man regret that the march of civilization has swept away the customs of the middle ages, and abolished the good old ordeal by battle. (A laugh.) I have confidence in the moderation of the Government, and I believe that, whichever way they may vote to-day, they at least will countenance no crusade against the squatters. I was going to say that I had faith in the Government; but perhaps if I did, I should be placed under wholesome restraint along with Koster. They tell me that too much faith is a bad thing nowadays; even too much faith in a Ministry. "*Cui neque apud Danaos usquam locus : insuper ipsi Dardanidæ infensi pænas cum sanguine poscunt.*"

On June 28th the policy of the Government was made a matter of censure, and Gordon made a few sensible remarks on the question :—

"Mr. Gordon had very little to say. He came to the House not exactly pledged to support the *ad valorem* duties and to oppose free distillation, but with very strong feelings on both questions. He was, however, he hoped, open to conviction ; yet so far he had no wish to abandon his former creed. In the present discussion he thought the question was more one of parties than of principles. The fiscal policy of the Government was not fairly before the House ; and he for one would prefer waiting until it was, before either approving or condemning the Ministers. The Government might not be agreed amongst themselves ; but by allowing them time they might be able to adjust their differences, and to present a policy which would be that of the whole Cabinet. He demurred to the notion that on this question members ought to be compelled to vote according to their avowed political opinions. The subject was not properly before the House, and he would vote for the previous question."

On July 5th a question arose about the erection

of a Post Office at Kincraig, South Australia. Gordon took the side of the inhabitants, and said they "had on one hand a petition signed by 43 inhabitants, and on the other a petition signed by Mr. Peter Prankerd, a land broker. If appeared that he had purchased nearly one-fourth of the township of Narracoorte for himself and principals, and expressed a hope that the buildings would not be erected to suit the views of private speculators. Was he not a private speculator? He was not one who would rob Peter to pay Paul, but he would rather comply with the request of the inhabitants than consult the wishes of Mr. Prankerd."

Desirous of benefiting his district by the stream of immigrants arriving in South Australia, Gordon, on July 12th, "asked the Commissioner of Crown Lands and Immigration, whether, in the event of residents in the South-East engaging immigrants on their arrival here, the Government will be prepared to defray the expenses of the same as far as Port MacDonnell or Robe. Under the present system the South-East derived little benefit from immigration, most of their labour being received from Victoria." The Government declined to adopt such a course without special authority.

On July 12th Gordon's colleague, Mr. Riddoch,

moved a resolution about the making of a main road at Mount Gambier. Gordon spoke as follows on the question :—

"Mr. Gordon thought the importance of the work could not be overrated. He had travelled over the line, which was the great outlet for the stream of traffic from Mosquito Plains and the neighbourhood, and was fully aware of the vile state it was in. It was exceedingly important that the roads necessary for carrying the produce of the district to market should be attended to. The money already granted for the line from Mount Gambier to Port MacDonnell would do wonders, and if the line was made passable as far as Penola the amount of traffic would be doubled in consequence of the development it would effect in the trade. He thought that the construction of works of this nature would justify the incurring of a small debt ; but, as it was, they had, as the French would say, an *embarras de richesses*, which they could not more wisely expend than in opening up lines of communication. He would not go into the question of the roads in the South-East generally ; but when they bore in mind that during the last half-dozen years more than half a million of money had been obtained from the sale of lands in the district, and when they reflected that there was still a large amount of land lying

ready to replenish the public coffers, he thought it
could not be said that too much was being asked
for the South-East. On the occasion of the former
discussion——

" The Chairman—The hon. member must not
refer to a former debate.

" Mr. Gordon said he had heard from the hon.
member Mr. Milne a remark which reminded him
of something he had heard before, to the effect
that nothing more should be heard in the South-
East District with regard to annexation and so on.
When he came to the House first he found on his
table a pamphlet bearing on the subject of annexation, and no doubt it was very entertaining, but
he had not read it yet, and he did not think it
likely he would. There was no doubt, however,
judging from the local paper, that there were
some clever literary men at Mount Gambier. He
hoped the Government would consider this motion
favourably, and that no opposition would be offered
to it in the House."

On October 3rd Gordon seconded the adoption
of the Address in reply to the Governor's Speech
in the following brief terms :—

" He was not aware that he could offer anything additional to the very full remarks of the
hon. mover, who had, in his opinion, said enough
for them both. (A laugh.) He did not feel

capable of speaking upon the policy of the country
at large, and quite agreed that they wanted no
taxation except perhaps a tax on wire fencing. (A
laugh.) ”

On November 3rd Gordon treated the House
to one of his “ classical-mythological ” speeches.
The Government had been attacked for its appointment of Mr. H. E. Downer as Commissioner
of Insolvency. *Hansard* reports as follows :—

“ Mr. Gordon preferred that the motion should
be met in a straightforward way to meeting it by
resorting to the previous question. When he
came into the House he had no intention of
speaking to the question, but since it had assumed
a hostile shape he thought it well to say a few
words. He was not acquainted at all with the
gentleman named in the notice, but regarding it
as a hostile motion he would speak accordingly.
He was rather astonished last session at a remark
of an hon. member now in office, but then on the
other side of the House, to the effect that the
Government of the day had been exposed to
nothing like such attacks as their predecessors
were subjected to. Well, scarcely a week passed
this session before a vote of censure was brought
forward, and certainly if that was mere child's
play the position of the present Ministry might be
regarded as a most unenviable one. (Laughter.)

He could not see the utility of such ceaseless strife, which tended to impede the progress of business indefinitely. The Opposition were like the heads of the Hydra — *Quique redundabat fœcundo vulnere serpens ;* and like the spearsman on the field of Flodden—

> " ' Each stepping where his comrade stood
> The instant that he fell.'

(Laughter.) The principle of the *lex talionis* was of course recognized to a great extent, and those who were ejected from office did not feel much leniency towards their successors ; but he trusted that the independent members who did not take office—simply perhaps from there being no chance of their obtaining it—(laughter)—would set their faces against these frequent changes, which could not but prove injurious to the welfare of the colony. There was once in England, he believed, a gentleman who made himself conspicuous as a king-maker during the wars between the Houses of York and Lancaster. He came to grief somewhere, which was rather a pity, for he was a decent sort of a man in spite of his peculiar habit of mind. But what he wished to say was that they might do better than the Earl of Warwick, who could scarcely be regarded as a good leader, seeing that he could not even support

Governments of his own creating. (Hear and a
laugh.) He did not wish to bring historical
parallels of too old a date, but he would say that
if Macaulay was right in saying that the Cavaliers
fought with the Roundheads in a neighbourly and
courteous manner, the same could not be said of
political antagonists. If theirs was a civil war it
certainly was not very polite, and the way they
went about it was not likely to promote harmony
and good feeling, or, as the member for Light
would say, 'conviviality.' (Hear and laughter.)
He did not regret having recorded a silent vote
the other day on the motion of the hon. member
Mr. Townsend, and he was quite ready to defend
it on political grounds; but it appeared to him
that the words '*Tros Tyriusque mihi nullo discrimine
agetur*' applied, which might be freely translated—
'East Adelaide and West Torrens are all one to
me, and I shall support what measures I approve of, from whatever source they may come.'
(Laughter.) He believed the difficulty of forming
Ministries arose not from a dearth of talent in the
House, but from a superfluity of that article.
(Hear, hear, and laughter.) They were oppressed
with an *embarras de richesses*, and he threw out
this suggestion for what it was worth, namely,
that the Treasury benches should be enlarged,
if only to give accommodation to a few super-

numeraries. (Laughter.) With regard to the question before the House—(Hear, hear)—he would say that the fame of Mr. Downer had not yet reached the South-East, but he should oppose the motion, as it was a hostile one. He intended to support the Government whenever he could fairly do so, always giving them the benefit of the doubt where doubt existed."

On December 20th a question of road-making in the Mount Gambier district again occupied the attention of the House. Gordon said " he would not detain the House with many remarks. The Chief Secretary wanted to turn them over to the tender mercies of the Central Road Board, who were going to spend £16,660 16s. 4d. on the district. But he held that was far too small a sum for such an important district. The House ought to look not merely at what they got out of the district, but at the resources which were still within it. (Hear.) There were several large and flourishing towns in it; it had fine rich agricultural land, and all that was needed for its development was a free expenditure on roads. Whatever steps were taken to facilitate the connection of the district with the capital would be for the good of the colony at large. He did not think they ought to be dependent on the Road Board. He thought the people in Adelaide did not appreciate the value of the trade in the districts, or they would be more disposed to do them justice."

On January 10, 1866, a motion in Gordon's name concerning the holding of Circuit Courts in his district lapsed through his absence. On January 16th he made a few unimportant observations on the work performed by local magistrates.

On February 1st the Adelaide members desired the House to grant money for various city improvements, and in the course of debate some reference was made to a supposed antagonism between town and country members. Gordon said:

"He did not think that the country members entertained any antagonistic feeling to the city, and in proof of this he should vote for the motion, not inquiring too closely whether it would be laid out in ornamental or useful works. Adelaide was not too beautiful; but with regard to some of the country districts, embellishment was quite superfluous. So far as Mount Gambier was concerned, to try to ornament it would be something like the attempt to 'paint the lily and adorn the rose.' All that was wanted there were works of utility."

On February 9th Gordon moved the following resolution:—

" ' That in the opinion of this House it is expedient that local land sales be held at Mount Gambier, in the South-East District.'

" He said the motion was one of importance, and it had been discussed for some time back amongst the people in the South-East, but no action had been taken. It had been argued that land brought a higher price when sold in the capital ; but that argument would not hold good now. He believed it would bring higher prices in Mount Gambier than in Adelaide. At a private land sale on the 7th a good portion brought £12 10s. per acre, which was a large price. Farmers in the neighbourhood had always a little money to lay out in land, and would give a fair price. It was not always convenient to travel to Adelaide, and there was a natural dislike to employ agents. These agents, any more than other persons, could not serve two masters, and they might get commissions from different persons to purchase the same land. The question was which place was best for the country. Now, there could be no doubt that it was better that the land should get into the hands of persons who wanted it, and would occupy it, than into those capitalists who would do nothing with it. He could not say with the hon. member Mr. Bright that he hoped to satisfy all persons by his motion, but he believed he would the majority."

14

The Government opposed the motion, but were defeated on division.

From this time up to September 26th, Gordon, although frequently attending the sittings of the House, and voting in numerous divisions, made no speeches worth reporting. On September 26th his colleague moved a resolution asking for monetary aid for the erection of a Mechanics' Institute at Mount Gambier. Gordon said :

" He had no wish to take advantage of the feeling of the House towards the district, which had of late been very liberal. There was a time when the South-East District was not so well known as at present, and last session a member of the House, who held a seat on the Treasury benches, referring to the local land sales in the district, remarked that the sales at Port MacDonnell would not benefit the people of Mount Gambier any more than the sales in Adelaide. That hon. member made a slight mistake in his knowledge of the geography of the place, for the two localities were much nearer than he could have supposed. He thought the district was entitled to some little consideration because of its position. He did not think the question should be looked at in its moneyed aspect, so much as respect to the advantages to be derived from the establishment of a Mechanics'

Institute, which in a growing population could not be overrated."

Later on in the debate an hon. member accused the South-Eastern District (of which Gordon was one of the representatives) of thinking that all their demands should be granted. Gordon remarked :

" The members for the South-East had never yet brought forward any such ,argument as that. (Hear.) The people of the South-East were, he believed, desirous of uniting themselves more and more closely to South Australia, but they were in an isolated position, and had many difficulties to contend against. All the money laid out to facilitate access with Mount Gambier was barely sufficient to counteract the disadvantages arising from the tract of uncultivated and useless desert which separated them from the metropolis. Being so near to the Victorian boundary they were, to a certain extent, drawn towards the neighbouring colony, whatever might be their good intentions towards this province. The Hon. Mr. Strangways said he remembered the time when a proposition of this sort would not have been entertained. No doubt he did, for it was only lately that the South-East had come into prominent notice. He thought there was a marked distinction between voting money for Mechanics' Institutes and for Rifle

Associations and Queen's Hundreds, for in the former case the object was to promote education and to foster a love of knowledge in the breast of the labouring classes, who, during election times, were befriended by everybody."

On September 28th Gordon made a few unimportant remarks on a question relating to the Adelaide Hospital. From this time forward his attendance became more intermittent, and speech-making was abandoned. On October 26th a " call of the House " was made, and it is recorded that " Mr. Gordon was the only member who did not answer nor excuse his absence." No record of any subsequent attendance is to be found, but on November 20, 1866, the following incident took place.

"REPRESENTATION OF VICTORIA.

" The Speaker reported receipt of a letter from Mr. A. L. Gordon, resigning his seat as a representative of the District of Victoria.

" The Chief Secretary (Hon. A. Blyth) moved that a vacancy has occurred in the representation in this House of the District of Victoria by the resignation of A. L. Gordon, Esq., and that the Speaker do forthwith issue his writ to supply such vacancy.

" Carried."

It may be interesting to refer to some of the
routine legislative work performed by Gordon
during his brief Parliamentary existence. He presented the following petitions. From the inhabitants of Kincraig, Narracoorte, and Penola,
against the declaration of a hundred in the district; from 139 residents of Mount Gambier West,
praying that the reserved land round Mount
Gambier and the Lakes, together with the old
telegraph station, might be placed under the jurisdiction of the District Council; from 240 inhabitants of Mount Gambier and the South-Eastern
District, praying for the erection of an hospital at
Mount Gambier; from residents of Mount Gambier, &c., having reference to Land Sales, Circuit
Court, Immigration, Impounding Act, &c. In
divisions his vote is recorded on the following
questions :—With the successful Noes against
" an instruction to the Select Committee on
Waste Lands, to inquire into and report on the
advisability, or otherwise, of selling, instead of
leasing, the mineral lands of the colony"; with
the successful Ayes on the Third Reading of the
Court of Appeals Amendment Act, 1865; with the
successful Ayes on the Third Reading of the
Miners Bill, 1865; with the successful Noes
against a resolution making " it desirable that
the Crown lands to be offered for sale at the

Government Land Sales should be classified, and different upset prices affixed according to the value of such lands"; with the successful Noes against State subsidised tramways; with the successful Noes against an amendment on the Licensed Victuallers Amendment Bill "to close public houses entirely on the Sabbath, except for bonâ fide travellers"; with the unsuccessful Ayes in favour of the amendment: "Any person holding a publican's license shall be at liberty to close his house entirely on the Lord's Day;" with the successful Ayes for the presentation of an Address to the Queen "for the amotion of Mr. Justice Boothby;" with the successful Ayes in favour of voting £1,000 for the "purpose of improving the banks of the River Torrens." On September 4, 1866, he was elected to a committee to take evidence and report on the "best means of improving the means of internal communication in the South-Eastern portion of the province, by means of tram-road or otherwise." His share of the duties were unfulfilled.

The foregoing pages are a complete record of his public life as a Member of Parliament, and I trust will afford some measure of gratification to those who have hitherto known little or nothing of this period of the poet's life.

FINALE.

THUS ends, for the present, my labour of love. I little thought, twenty-two years ago—when, as a small boy, I looked up with reverential eyes at Adam Lindsay Gordon, in Collins Street, Melbourne—that my love for him as a poet, and my admiration of him as a man, would have grown sufficiently intense to prompt me to undertake a task so pleasant, and yet withal so regretful, as that which I now bring to a conclusion. In the foregoing pages I have made no attempt at elaboration, but have simply stated, as concisely as possible, the main facts of the poet's life, in the hope that their perusal may be an equal pleasure to other lovers of the poet as the task of their narration has been to me.

J. H. R.

www.ingramcontent.com/pod-product-compliance
Lightning Source LLC
Chambersburg PA
CBHW030131030726
47498CB00007B/2655